SCYLLA

THE REVENGE

This is a work of fiction. Names, characters,
places and incidents either are the product of
the author's imagination or are used
fictitiously, and any resemblance to any actual
persons, living or dead, events, or locales is
entirely coincidental.

Front cover artwork by Ms. Neyra Gomez
Back cover image provided by
Denny Rowland
5/15/2018

RockHill
Publishing LLC
PO Box 62241
Virginia Beach, VA 23466-
2241
www.rockhillpublishing.com

SCYLLA
THE REVENGE

BY MYRON EDWARDS

Table of Contents

Author's note

When I began to write about The Mistress of the Rock, I never thought that there would ever be more than one story to it. I was wrong. Cyprus has so many legends, myths, and magical places to visit and to learn about, that I am only just now starting to appreciate what a captivating and exciting island the place is.

That is why I would like to dedicate this second book to the people of Cyprus, and to The Island of Love.

I also would like to thank Lili Panagi of Pan Media, for her constant encouragement and support, Valerie Singleton, a life-long friend who always told me to keep going. James Hill of Rock Hill publishing, my publisher, and the brilliant editing skills of Athina Paris.

I would also like to thank the many, many people, who have encouraged me throughout the adventure and to those who bought Book One and left comments. Finally, I would like to thank my family; my wife Niki and my three children. They have been there in times of great stress and have always told me to keep going.

As I said, if you believe, there is no more to be said.

"Be aware, Mr. Cole, *The Mistress of the Rock is a possessive spirit she does not give her affections lightly.*"

"Do you remember that Richard?"

Richard Cole awoke suddenly, startled from his sleep. He rose slowly and sat on the edge of the bed, his body drenched in sweat.

His wife Julie lay beside him, blissfully unaware of his nightmare.

CHAPTER ONE

Cape Greco, Cyprus

Friday, 2:30pm

"Go on, what are you waiting for?"

Barry stood on the edge of the ancient, jagged, clifftop and looked down. Below him the glistening blue waters of the Mediterranean Sea cruised towards the rocks, creating small white horses of foam, which dipped, bubbled, and frothed, each one surging to shore on a carpet of fresh, bleached white waves. He looked down, and the sea bid him welcome.

'Come on, Barry. For Christ's sake, it's not that far. Just do it!' He shouted to no one except himself while stones underfoot bit into the bare flesh. He trod gingerly over the fine shingle and moved to the edge of the rocky outcrop. Once again, he peered down into the water.

His body shook as fear rose, but he wasn't a coward. He had once been a bouncer at a Luton nightclub, so this should be easy. Besides, he had come too far to back down now. After all, wasn't this his idea to jump from the cliffs? He looked down once more at the two bodies treading water thirty feet below.

Shutting his eyes, he ran forward, screamed "F U C K", and flung himself from the cliff and into the sea below.

Losing touch with the ground, his body felt weightless for the brief seconds it stayed in flight and keeping his eyes closed, he hurtled into the waves, his entry splash loud and large. The warm water hit him and came as a surprise to his numb body.

As he sank below the surface, one foot brushed against something and the Mediterranean gently caressed him. Reaching below the waves, he tugged at his shorts, which had slithered past his hips, and balanced precariously around his nether regions. One sharp pull corrected the problem, and he breast-stroked his way to shore, greeted cheerily by his fellow cliff jumpers.

Stepping ashore into the rocky outlet that housed the hermit caves of the past, the pungent odour of dead fish and stale urine wafted into his nostrils. Unfortunately, the caves doubled as a makeshift urinal, which, if you caught a whiff of the obnoxious scent, was most unpleasant for a popular tourist spot.

Chrissy, nineteen, an undergraduate and part-time barista at Starbucks, Muswell Hill, dried herself with her recently bought 'I love Cy' towel, and slapped Barry on the backside, her way of congratulating him. Barry responded by kissing her on top of her head. They had been together just over six months, the last-minute flight offer Barry spotted on the web, was their first holiday away together.

"What's that?" Chrissy was the first to notice the small piece of material stuck to Barry's toes, which had wrapped itself around the middle one.

Barry leaned down to poke at the material.

Mary and Greg, who had also been able to get time off and join them on their cheap flight, reached them.

Mary was taller than the boys and somewhat self-conscious of the fact; but she was a good laugh, with a wicked sense of humour, and fit, not only because her job as a fitness instructor in Islington Gym meant she kept herself supple, but she also looked good in all the right places, and together with her daily fitness routines ensured her skin tones and muscles stayed perfectly honed. Mary's rapidly tanning body made her bright blue eyes even more obvious against her flaxen blonde hair; she was undoubtedly the most striking of the four.

Greg, her man of the moment, completed the foursome. He was also blond and like the rest, in his early twenties. But Greg was just a bit thick academically, and not as qualified as the others were, with just a moderate education; nothing 'university or college' about Greg. But what he lacked academically he made up for in savvy, as he had finished his electrician's apprenticeship and was now pulling in more money than the other three. Greg was also looking to emigrate, with Australia as his preferred place. He hadn't told anyone about his plans and wasn't saying anything just yet about it to Mary; he wanted to see how the holiday went and make his move afterwards.

Barry pulled the piece of material from his toes and examined it closely, turning it around in his fingers.

"What is it?" Greg leaned down to prod at the piece as well.

"Not sure, but I think it's a bit of net. Probably a fishing net as it has some red stuff on it. Maybe blood from an unlucky fish that got caught. Just latched onto my foot." Barry threw the piece away and it nestled on one of the rocks below the water's edge. "That was so good, I am going to do it again. Who's coming with me?"

Barry's enthusiasm for the cliff jump wasn't greeted as warmly by the others.

"Alright, I'll go on my own." He gathered up his towel and flip-flops and began the short walk up to the winding steps that led to the cliffs. "You can wait for me, or I will see you back at the top."

Greg, still seated next to Mary, gave Barry muted applause as he strode purposefully up the stairs, the handclap sounding more like a one-flipper seal flapping, not a gesture of appreciation.

Barry reached the top of the steps with the sun beating heavily on his bare shoulders as he gazed across the landscape. No one else was around. Not one tourist, the area deserted. *'That's odd.'* He would have expected at least a few people milling about, as just a short distance from the steps, were the sun-blanched white walls of the small and very famous Church of Agioi Anargyroi, which was always a great tourist attraction and hub for the curious.

He caught a last glimpse of the church as the sun cut a long arrow-like shadow pointing along the pathway leading to the rocks. This time, there was no hesitation, save for him making sure his shorts were on tight. He made his way to the edge, and peered over once, checking that no one was below him. Preparing for the jump, he took three steps back, just as Mary, Greg, and Chrissy began their climb up the steps.

'They are going to miss it,' he grinned to himself, took off his flip-flops, and placed them close to a large stone on the rim of the cliff. Then taking one large deep breath, he ran. This time, he didn't scream as he threw himself off the edge and into the sea, his brief flight over in a couple of seconds.

Greg reached the top of the steps and looked over his shoulder. Although his vantage point to the bottom was not clear, from what he could tell, Barry had not yet surfaced. He waited for the girls; Mary arrived first, followed by Chrissy, and all three waited for Barry to emerge from the water.

Chrissy moved to the edge of the rock and called out, "Barry." There was silence, except for the distant echo of the waves as they crested towards the caves below.

Mary moved next to Chrissy and looked down, her extra couple of inches, she believed, an advantage when spotting for things, like missing friends. Both were wearing anxious and nervous expressions, sensing something was not right.

Chrissy moved to the exact spot where Barry had jumped from, and again, called out to him. Again, there was no reply. She shouted louder, and then louder still. Panic crept into her voice and her heart began to race. She looked down into the water below. All was quiet; very quiet, too quiet.

From her vantage point, Chrissy scanned the beach then turned away, missing the piece of material that had been previously attached to Barry's foot slip from the rocks, and float out into the waves.

Greg, now worrying about his friend too, reached into his bag, and pulled out his mobile phone. He waited a couple of minutes before pushing the numbers *112*, the universal European Emergency number.

Chrissy ran down the stairs and stood at the bottom, still looking out to sea, then summoning all her energy, raced back up the steps and stood looking over the cliff from where Barry had leapt. She bent down to pick up the pair of flip-flops, which he had so neatly positioned next to the large stone by the edge, ready for his return.

The ceiling fan in the small police station at Protaras worked overtime attempting to keep the room cool. Greg sat on a plain wooden chair. Hot and sweaty in the humid room, he waited for someone to enter; it had been an hour since his last visitor.

'Where are the girls and what the hell happened to Barry?' He wondered.

After he called the authorities, the local Cape Greco police responded quickly, with the first car and ambulance arriving in just under four minutes. The search was immediate, with a couple of guys in scuba equipment part of the entourage of searchers. He watched from his position as the hunt for Barry got underway, but it was clear after less than fifteen minutes that he was not in the water, or where he should have been.

Those first moments of panic seemed like a long time ago now as he stood up and took a few steps away from the chair. He looked around him at the graffiti-covered walls; most of the words were Greek names etched with biro, felt-tip, or just scratched on. He thought about adding his own but rejected the idea. He didn't want to be here at all, let alone leave a record of his visit.

A large Cypriot policeman in his late forties and a stout waistline, pushed his way through the door; his face was sweating, his armpits were sweating, in fact, most of his heavy faded uniformed blue shirt seemed damp. He wiped his face with a handkerchief, before taking his seat at the desk, slapped down papers, and faced Greg, who waited patiently while the man settled himself, and eventually looked up from the pile of papers.

"My Engleesh, it is not good. You want *nero*, water?"

Greg nodded and the man lumbered out of the room.

Greg was becoming uncomfortable and not simply because of the heat. The man was back within a minute and handed Greg a small plastic cup, which he downed in one gulp, the ice-cold water giving him little comfort from this unscheduled meeting. He sat down again looking around the room as the officer shuffled more papers from the heap in front of him.

An old standard analogue-style phone covered in stickers sat on the desk in front of the policeman. He tapped it lightly with his fingers and at once, it rang. He was obviously expecting a call, and now it came.

"Nai… Nai…" his tone rose and fell with each word, "Dora, nai, Εντάξει. Efcharisto." He put the phone down, turned to Greg, and pointed. "Περίμενε."

Greg had no idea what he said, but presumed it meant to stay where he was. The door opened and closed quickly.

Another man, bigger than Greg, entered. He wore a crisp white shirt, and on the top pocket was a monogrammed name, *Nicos,* embossed in black. He was slim-built and energetic looking, yet, he carried a cool, bordering on suave look to his posture. Around his neck and visible, due to his open shirt, was a heavy-looking gold Greek cross. There was not a trace of perspiration on him and just the faintest hint of cologne. He walked across to the now vacant desk and sat down.

His smart black trousers and shiny shoes complimented his appearance perfectly and matched his equally elegantly styled hair. His face looked young, and Greg guessed he could be no more than thirty, perhaps even younger, and he had an air about him that oozed confidence.

"My name is Detective Inspector Nicos Styllianou, C Division, Nicosia, Mr Haley."

It was the first time anyone had spoken Greg's name to him since he got there.

"So, tell me Mr Haley, what do you think has happened to your friend, Mr Rochester?"

Greg gazed at him, shrugged his shoulders, and gave a straight honest look that said no more than *'I haven't got a clue.'* "I'm sorry I don't know anything, except that he jumped off the cliff, and that was the last we saw of him."

"Did you actually see him jump?"

The Detective settled into his, what Greg could only assume, was the probing questions routine.

"No, not exactly, we heard him and then he was gone."

"You heard him jump off?"

"No. Well, no, not really…" Greg began to sweat more. The ceiling fan needed another speed. "Have you found him then?"

"Not yet, Mr Haley, but we will." He reached into his pocket and took out a slim packet of cigarettes.

All around the room were 'No Smoking' signs.

Greg smiled, *'Even the police break the rules here.'*

Nicos leaned down and switched on his fake cigarette. "Old habits, Mr Haley."

Greg smiled again, he didn't really care what habits the man had, he just wanted out of there.

"So, the last time you saw Mr Rochester was when he jumped off the cliff, and you didn't see him after that?"

"Right, yes, but we went looking. Chrissy, Barry's girlfriend, ran down the steps to see if he was pissing about, then she ran back again and told me he wasn't anywhere to be seen, by then I had already called you, the police, that is. They got to us quick I have to say."

Nicos ignored the slanted compliment. "Yes, this is what your friends told me." He stood up and dragged on his fake cigarette. "What do you think happened, Mr Hayley?"

"As I said, I don't know." Greg looked again at the detective as if trying to read his thoughts. Did he believe him; or did he think there was more to the story than what he said?

"That is all for now, Mr Hayley. When are you returning to the UK?"

"Next Wednesday, we arrived two days ago."

"It is possible we will need to speak to you before then, so don't leave town, as they say."

Greg didn't fully appreciate Nicos's flippant remark, as he stood, and shook the offered hand. "Are we suspects then?"

"Everyone is a suspect, until we prove they are not. But don't let this spoil your holiday, I am sure Mr Rochester will be found very quickly."

Nicos's smile didn't reassure Greg of anything.

"Please, don't worry too much, these things happen." The inspector's demeanour had changed in a few sentences, becoming almost amicable. "Oh, one further thing, Mr Haley…"

Greg sensed the Columbo moment.

"How loud was the splash? It may give us some idea of where he landed, as the locals know that area so well."

Greg thought for a second, replaying instantly those moments in his mind. "I didn't hear a splash." He fixed his eyes on the man.

"Yes, that is what your friends said as well. Don't you find that strange? I do. Your friend jumps from say, thirty feet, into the sea, and no splash. Very odd. No matter, we shall look into this further. You may go now, Mr Haley."

Greg walked to the end of the short corridor, where Mary and Chrissy sat waiting on a short wooden bench. Chrissy's eyes were red; she had been crying, a lot.

Friday and Saturday nights in Protaras were not as loud as Ayia Napa. True, it had its fair share of bars, restaurants, and clubs, but the clientele was generally older than the "Napa" crowd, more hip and pop than hip and hop.

The British influence in Protaras, ran throughout the town with notable names like *Only Fools and Horses* and the *Wellington and Robin Hood* pubs, and other assorted 'Brit' bars and restaurants dotted about. All great places for good food, good beer, and good Karaoke, but that might also depend on who was doing the singing. Most of the wannabes had reasonable voices but they were all lacking the X Factor. But none of that mattered to the three young people who sat on the edge of *Filo's bar* drinking. For this trio, it had been two hours since they had left the police station, after which, copious amounts of alcohol were consumed by all three. Brandy sour glasses stacked in twos filled the small table at the Cafe.

As they sat drinking and thinking, groups of people walked past them into the small hours, and onto their beds, but for Chrissy, Greg, and Mary, watching, drinking, and waiting was the order of the night as they waited for the call or text to announce that their friend had been found.

But since leaving the station, no one had heard a thing about Barry and it was now mere speculation what had happened to him, and although the dreaded question was never asked, everyone knew what it was.

Frimley, Friday, 9pm

Myron Edwards

Richard sat at the kitchen table with the ceiling fan spinning round and round at half speed. Sipping his coffee, he began to read the newspaper in front of him. The headlines all seemed to be the same day after day. Another package of austerity measures for Cyprus, Greece, and Portugal, "Spain teeters on brink…" Next to the doom, came the boom, with celebrities packing yet another film première, prancing down the red carpet and teasing the paparazzi.

CHAPTER TWO

Hell hath no fury

Frimley, Saturday morning
Richard sat at his laptop, all references to Aphrodite and the Rock wiped clean from the machine. The screensaver showed his two kids, just before they had set off on their joint world trip. The original plan of Molly going solo, changed when Matthew announced that he would like to join her. This delighted Julie; Molly would be much safer with her big brother tagging along.

The two had begun their journey to the US, starting with New York, before making their way across the states to LA, where they caught a plane to Tokyo, Japan. They stayed only a few days there as they found it expensive and needed to find work quickly if they were not to go globe-trotting with only a few pounds in their pockets.

They chose Thailand and settled on the beach resort of Phuket; their last email to Julie confirming that was where they were presently. In it, the news was, Matthew had found a job working on the beach with a parasailing Aussie, whom he had struck up a guy-thing with, and Molly was at an Ex-Pat restaurant called *Benny's*, the owner being a huge Benny Hill fan. Molly liked the work but loathed the theme they seemed to play all day long, especially at birthday parties. The other thing that made her smile and sometimes giggle was when tourists, usually from the States, kept calling the resort "Fuck It", instead of pronouncing it Phuket. She tried to explain how it should be pronounced, POO KET, but somehow it seemed funnier the way they said it and just a little risqué; typical Benny Hill, he would have loved it.

Julie checked her watch; any minute now they would call for an update, the local time in Thailand just about 5pm. Every Saturday since the start of the journey, Molly, or Matthew called around this time to let them know how things were. This being the only thing Richard had insisted upon. And just like clockwork, the phone rang.

Julie, let it ring once, before grabbing it. "Hello, darling…" Her Bostonian twang elevated with each word.

Richard sat in the kitchen chair listening, smiling, and making gestures with his hands, which Julie ignored, or when she remembered he was looking at her, smiled back at him.

He sensed a tingle around his ears, and knew they were probably glowing red as he felt himself being pulled towards his wallet. But as he listened, he also heard another voice, one that up until that morning had not been heard for nearly a year. The hairs on his neck stood erect, and goose bumps shimmered down his arms.

"Look what I did, Richard. Look what I did." The voice, no more than a whisper, penetrated his soul.

He looked around, the voice so clear, its owner could have been standing in the room.

Julie was still ensconced in her conversation with their daughter.

The voice was gone, but the message remained.

Turning to his laptop, he found Google search, and typed in *Cyprus news*. He selected, surreptitiously, a page on Cyprus Mail. Julie looked over to him and he discreetly turned the screen away from her glance. He scanned the first page, mostly dedicated to the ongoing Euro bailout and financial crisis that gripped the island. Next, he skimmed an article about the protracted negotiations for Hydro-Carbon exploration Cyprus was developing, which offered a ray of light in a dark economy. Then his heart skipped a beat. He found a small paragraph at the very bottom with the headline; *Tourist goes missing after cliff Jump in Cape Greco.*

"Yes, Richard. Read it, see what I have done." The voice urged him.

His stomach churned as he began to read the news item but to his disappointment, Julie ended her call. He moved off the page and back to the BBC website. He needed to re-read that in peace. Then he snapped back to the conversation. "All okay, are they?"

"Yes, fine. I will send them some cash, just for some little extras, okay?"

There wasn't much he could say against it. Besides, he wanted to get Julie out so he could read more about the missing tourist. "Why don't you go to the post office, then you can send it right away and they will get it by Thursday. The Post office is open now, and it shouldn't be that busy; it's not a pensioner's day, is it?"

"Are you trying to get rid of me?" Julie leaned towards the screen. "What are you looking at, porn?"

"Porn, me? Why would I look at virtual women when I have the real thing?"

The compliment worked a treat. "Let me have the bank card, I will use that."

He opened his wallet, fished for the card, which was hidden behind a pile of petrol receipts, and handed it over.

She kissed him on the cheek, put her coat on, and picked up her car keys. "Oh, and I might get some new shoes; I saw a pair earlier this week, just gorgeous they were." With that, she was out of the back door.

He waited for the car to leave before returning to the page on the missing tourist. His coffee was stone-cold, but still he took a sip. It tasted bitter and he almost spat it out, before reluctantly swallowing the cold liquid. He moved down the page and read the complete report. Apparently, this was not the first person to go missing either; a young Romanian boy, aged nine, had also met the same fate, believed drowned over ten days ago, and still not found. Moving off that page, he went to the search engine to find more details on the report.

It had happened in Cape Greco so he went to the Ayia Napa Gazette page, opened it, and read the bolder headline. This one spoke of two missing persons but did not list the names. As he sat reading, he felt as if someone stood behind him, looking over his shoulder. He could also smell something sweet, like lavender, only, there were no flowers in the kitchen or air freshener that smelled like that. He turned around slowly, his fear betraying his senses. There was nothing there.

"You spurned me once, Richard, not again." Her voice was back in his head.

The voice he had cut out of his consciousness and dared to believe would never be heard again was back. But this time, it seemed darker, malevolent, and far more sinister. It penetrated his mind, slowly twisting, and grinding, as if turning a screw inside his head. He could almost feel the blood pulse from the wound as her words dug deeper.

"You, Richard, will do my bidding. You will obey me, because this I promise you, if you do not, as they say in your world, 'Hell hath no fury like a woman scorned'." There was a brief pause before she continued. Her sentences were well-defined, thought-out, and delivered for greatest effect. *"Can you imagine the sheer hell and pain I can bring you and your family as a goddess? Dying would be an easy way out of the agony but that I won't allow you to do. Oh no, Richard Cole, dying is not on my agenda for you."*

"What do you want me to do?" His plea to an unknown presence made the scenario even more absurd but there was no denying the look of sheer terror he now carried as he waited for her words, which were just two.

"Not yet."

Drinking what was left of the cold coffee, he swallowed it without thought or complaint. He stood up, paced back and forth in the medium-sized kitchen, opened cupboards, and peaked inside, as if searching for answers. Then, he returned to the laptop, closed the page, and switched it off just as Julie's car revved and pulled into the driveway.

He needed to stay calm, not give Julie cause for his suspicious behaviour, because the ruse of porn-watcher would only last a little longer. But how could he tell her that hell was about to be unleashed upon them again? Yes, he lied before, but only to protect her. Now, it seemed he would have to do it again.

What if he just told her the truth, just came out with it? After all, she was present when the bitch Aphrodite made her last appearance. She had seen what he had and what he felt. Still, he wasn't sure. Possibly, he needed to wait for the right moment.

Frimley, Hyper Market, Saturday afternoon
The car had been squeezed into the middle parking aisle at the hyper-market. It was the only space left, as the store was always busy and full of bargain hunters after the two-for-one offers. Waiting for Julie, he began loading the shopping into the car, as she took the trolley back to claim her one pound. Closing the boot, he saw the goddess' reflection on the paintwork and heard her voice in his head.

"I am waiting, Richard. Know this, people will suffer if you don't come to me soon, innocent people."

He opened the boot again and slammed it down hard.

Julie looked over towards him as she returned with her pound clutched in her hand. "You okay?" She smiled and waited for his reply.

"Yes, fine. Boot got stuck, that's all. No worry, let's go." He opened the door for her and climbed into the driver's seat.

But the voice in his head began to speak again. He tried to cut it out by smiling at Julie and started a conversation. "We did okay today, a few bargains."

"Why are you ignoring me, Richard? You know what I'm capable of. How many more people must die before you listen?" She continued to torment.

Richard's conversation was drivel, but it was all he could muster; *'try to make it mundane and keep that bitch out of my head,'* he assured himself.

But her influence was too powerful, as she continued to spike his thoughts. *"You are not listening, Richard. I want you to listen."* Her voice became more insistent.

He turned the corner and the wheels caught the kerb. "Sorry." He apologised and looked across to Julie then smiled awkwardly as she sat belted in her seat. He reached across to take her hand.

"Richard, the road!"

Julie's sharp admonishment focused his attention back on the task at hand.

"I am losing my patience, and next time, it might not be strangers. Maybe I will look for someone a little closer to home; do you understand me? Do you understand what I mean by closer to home?"

He put his foot down and tried to drive the voice from his head.

"Slow down, Richard, it's only thirty here. What on earth is the matter?" Julie was becoming increasingly uneasy.

And he sensed it.

"They say Thailand is nice this time of the year, although, it can suffer from terrible Tsunamis."

The implied threat to his children made him scream inside. How could she throw threats around like this? She was only a figment of his imagination. He conjured her up. Now, he had to get rid of her. He turned the wheel and drove down the road towards their house.

Small water droplets began to fall on the windscreen, then became heavier, but he ignored the rain, and the wipers, preferring to peer through the blurred glass.

"You do have wipers."

Julie's pragmatism for the obvious was just what he needed to deflect his attention. He turned them on, just as the rain splashed heavier across the windscreen.

He had not heard the voice for a few hours, but he was sure she would be back soon enough. He started thinking of ways to meet the goddess' demands and knew instantly that the solution lay in returning to Cyprus. But how could he do that without raising Julie's suspicion? She had sworn to never go back, and he agreed; now, he had to break that promise. The way he saw it, there was only one avenue to follow and he wasn't even sure it would work. He checked his mobile numbers and found the name he needed.

"Jules, going out to get some petrol. I saw we were a bit light and I should have bought some at the hyper-market. It's cheaper there."

His conversation was mere words, words he needed to use to justify his actions as if he were already in covering-his-tracks mode. The subterfuge in these circumstances was infectious as one lie led straight into another, but still he had to make certain he didn't create suspicion, until he was ready to say something concrete.

Julie just nodded as he came down the stairs and opened the front door.

He smiled back at her, made his way out to the drive, and climbed into the car. He started the engine; the petrol indicator showed half a tank. He pulled out of the driveway, into the road, and sped away through the gears. He drove for about a mile then pulled over into a parking bay outside a row of shops opposite the garage. There, he took out his cell, pressed the digits, and waited.

"Hello… Christ, Richard, is that you? How have you been? Where have you been? It must be a year since…"

Peter's voice was not what Richard expected, although, if he were honest, he wasn't sure what reaction he would get.

At first, he tried to keep the conversation normal, even bordering on a neighbourly chat, but he needed something more than that from his pal. He needed assistance. "I'm fine… yes, we are fine. No, Pete, that is not true… we, are not, fine… I need your help."

"What's up? You know I haven't got much money. Sheila almost cleaned me out and the house isn't sold yet, so I'm staying in Paphos at a mate's flat. He's gone back to the UK for about a year since this financial crisis blew up, so I'm basically house-sitting. Anyway, you sound awful. What is it?"

"Pete, I need your help."

"You said that, what do you need?"

"I have to come to Cyprus."

"What? After what happened last time, that is not a good idea. And there are a few people around here who don't think a lot about you."

"Well, yes, I guessed as much, but I have to come. It's difficult to explain now, but I will try to do so when I get over. In the meantime, I need you to do something for me."

"Okay." Peter sat on the chair in his flat, listening.

"Remember you had some papers drawn up for Goddess Dives? I need you to call me tomorrow and say the Cypriot authorities are going to take you to court over tax non-payment. Therefore, you need me to fly over and act on your behalf. To declare me as the owner, and not you. I will then say I need my accountant to verify amounts, and you say that's fine, but insist that they need to see me in person."

"What's going on, Richard?"

"I'm not exactly sure but if I don't come over, I'm afraid of what might happen. I know it's a lot to ask but you have to trust me on this. So, please, will you do this for me?" His insistence was obvious, the tone, pleading.

"Okay, but I hope there is nothing illegal in this."

"No, nothing, I promise. I just need this excuse for getting there and this is the only thing I could think of…" Richard paused. "I will have to lie to Julie again, but I have no other choice. Okay then, tomorrow, at about this time. And thanks, I owe you."

"A crate of Keo would be nice."

"Yes, sure, first round on me. Take care and speak to you tomorrow." He sat back, took a long deep breath, started the car, and drove back to the house without filling the tank.

Ayia Napa, Saturday, 11:30pm

Night fishing had always been good around the waters of Ayia Napa. Once outside the harbour and away from the noise and fun of the island's trendiest resorts, there was a real feel of quiet relaxation, as the small motorboat bobbed up and down in the water whilst the sea gilded its bow. Two expensive fishing rods dangled over the side, their lines extended far out, and poised for action.

The half-moon glistened across the top of the still water; casting broken yellow streaks over the waves cutting through the darkness. The only other objects breaking the tranquillity and blackness were two glowing yellow neon floats that dipped in and out, seeking their prey.

The two tourist fishermen, both experienced and adept at their sport, cradled against the edge of the craft. It was one of those 'hire me out for fifty Euros a day' touches, definitely not complete with all the mod-cons, but sufficiently comfortable for the two of them. Here, they would try for the catch of the day, which was usually tuna, and ranged in weight from five to sixty pounds.

The waters around this coast teemed with silver fish, sea bream, dentex, pandora, parrotfish, red mullet, cardinal fish, moray eels, octopus, barracudas, and turtles throughout the year, but tuna was the definitive goal of the day for the two men and to take the edge off the colder than usual night air, they sipped a large bottle of Brandy between themselves. By morning, they could both be pissed.

The skipper was a local man, Demetrio. He had been a fisherman for most of his working life but found it particularly difficult after his second coronary. These days, he preferred the pleasure-boat style of fishing, leaving all the hard work to his clients.

As the two on deck drank, chatted, and joked, a slight sea mist began to coat the waves. It whirled across them like small puffs of white breath then just as suddenly as it appeared, it vanished. As the two sipped slowly from the bottle, the first line nearest the bow jerked, and jerked again, the float disappeared, and then the line crackled. The men sprang to their feet.

Joseph, the taller of the two, pulled slowly on the line, whilst Henry, his companion, and considerably shorter and wider, watched eagerly as Joseph grabbed hold of the fishing rod, before easing himself into his chair, and strapping himself in tight. He paused, not really knowing what was dangling on the other end of the line. Both were in their late 60's and not cut out for a long struggle, but this seemed like a good catch and the adrenaline was flowing.

Taking the rod in his hands, Joseph pulled slowly then almost gingerly, pulled again. As he reeled in, gradually taking the slack, the click-clack of the reel cut through the night's silence as the line began tightening. Henry and Demetrio watched, anticipating a great catch, as the action unfolded.

Joseph played the line through his hands. It was sharp, too sharp, as the tension straightened it and he tried to keep it still. Another click and a final clack, before he attacked, gripping the rod, and pulling hard. Then jerking the rod and line forward, the thing below the water broke to the surface.

At first, Joseph couldn't make it out as he struggled, and dragged the shape towards the boat.

Demetrio, sensing the capture and with a big smile on his face, took his boat hook and pushed it out towards the object, catching it, and then dragged it closer. But as it got closer to the small vessel, it became quite obvious what it was, and it was then that Joseph threw up.

Demetrio looked over the side, away from the other two, and whispered on the waves. "Panayia, Mother of God!"

CHAPTER THREE

Death, is quick in Cyprus

Nicosia, Sunday, 7pm
Elena Petrakis was the youngest of the three pathologists at the Nicosia Morgue; she was also the keenest and always eager to get her examinations done quickly and efficiently.

Death in Cyprus is usually a quick thing too, as most people are buried within twenty-four hours of their demise, and that procedure is one of ritual. If it is a villager's death, then the entire parish turns out and the grieving process starts with wailing and bell-tolling. The service begins and at times, the coffins are open, and sometimes are closed; it is for many, a matter of personal choice. The service consists of incense burning and numerous incantations, after which, the corpse is taken to its grave but not before more incense and a good plate smashing; with the coffin lid removed and the body on full display before being lowered into its final resting place. The lid is also ceremonially smashed and put beside the open casket. At this point, both mourners and grave diggers hurriedly come together to shovel the dirt as quickly as they can to cover the deceased before the elements can get to them.

Yes, death is quick in Cyprus, but in the case of Elena and the body before her, this one was not going anywhere anytime soon.

Death was not an alien thing to her, she had seen it in all its most gruesome forms, many times. Even for her young years, it was a daily occurrence, especially after the carnage of a late-night Saturday crash on the motorway. Indeed, those were the most upsetting, but as she pulled the sheet from the cadaver that lay in front of her, she reached for her camera and began to shoot the subject without hesitation; to say she was fascinated was the understatement of the week.

As she put down the camera, she prised back some of the loose flesh from the torso; fish had nibbled at most of the internal organs and the belly was bloated from the amount of seawater it had consumed. The legs also appeared broken and twisted, with the knee jutting out through an open gash on the right thigh. Elena moved her white rubber gloved hands up and over the body slowly; long deep lacerations scarred the chest, leaving thick black lines from the clotted blood that had once flowed through the youngster's veins. His arms, both right and left were badly bruised as if the body had been thumped or squeezed against something.

She moved from the body to the neck, which, on closer examination, confirmed that it had also been broken, snapped, and snapped again. Shifting to the left side of the body, she gently turned the top of the head; the features were certainly those of an Eastern European. The hair, though caked in blood, was brown and quite thick, his left eye remained closed, and the left side of his face while cut and scratched was still fairly intact. She moved around the table to the other side of his face. Her shocked expression confirming the sight that greeted her. For this was something she had not seen before. Where the boy's scalp and face should be, there was just a deep hole, nothing else, the cavity filled with cerebral matter and congealed blood. This part of the skull crushed into pulp. Moving closer to the gaping hole, she probed the puss, which had formed around the wound, with a small incisor. It leaked then bled and finally dripped and kept on dripping down to the floor. Creating a small pool of matter beside her feet.

This was something she had never seen before and to have it done to a young child, who not too long ago had been full of life, was something she could not comprehend.

Elena sat down on the stool by the desk as the liquid continued to drip, then took out her pen and began to make notes as she raised the camera and took three quick shots. She knew she had to examine this body properly, but not yet.

The florescent light in the corridor flickered then came on full; it was time for coffee.

As she moved to cover the corpse, she noticed the boy's shorts were torn in shreds and just the inner netting was left on him; his genitals crushed inside his body. She moved her hand over the material, one neat square was cut out or sliced from the net.

Why, among all this carnage, had someone taken the time to cut a small square out of the netting? It was a question Elena had no idea how to answer, for all it kept doing was making her ask more questions. She turned the light off in the morgue and shut the door, locking it from the outside.

Nicos Styllianou received the call and put down his small cup of Greek coffee. He switched off the PC in front of him and picked up his notebook.

It was not far to the morgue and the drive would take only ten minutes, at most. Thankfully, the city was not as busy at this time of year. He grabbed his jacket and made his way towards the car park.

In the quiet village of Orounta in Nicosia district, Spyro Petrides, switched off the TV and made his way up the stairs to his bedroom. The old set buzzed, as it had always done for the last ten years. He climbed the last step and opened the bathroom door, his last-minute routine would see him do what he needed to do before climbing naked into his bed as he had done for the past thirty-five years. Only, in the last six months, instead of having a nice warm woman to cuddle next to, he had a cold spot on the bed where she should have been, had it not been for the cancer that ravaged her body and finally took her away.

Spyro looked around the empty room, at his empty life; all he clung to were memories. He pulled the white sheet back as he climbed into the bed, before drawing it over him. These days, he went to bed early, sleeping between four and five hours, and that included getting up a couple of times during the night, trying to return to slumber land before his day started all over again with his early morning deliveries.

Orounta had been his home for all these years but it felt more like a family as everyone knew everyone else. During the time of his loss, it was all he had left and that was something he treasured; the warmth and support of his village, because when someone died in their midst it was like they all lost a member of their own family. That was how close they were.

Spyro closed his eyes, as a lone stray dog barked long into the night.

The hospital was brightly lit as Nicos pulled into the car park. Two ambulances had just unloaded another batch of unwilling customers into the emergency department, flanked by a growing number of anxious relatives who grouped around the swing doors, some with cigarettes lit, puffing frantically. Nicos walked towards the rear of the building and took the stairs down to the long corridor that led to the morgue. He checked to see if the door was locked then turned and made his way further up the corridor, towards the canteen, where he saw Elena seated, drinking coffee, and having a cigarette.

Nicos felt tempted to take out his own nicotine substitute, but refrained, then sat down beside her, planting a small kiss on both cheeks, Mediterranean style. "Yasso, Tikanis?"

"Kala, Isi?" Elena returned his traditional greeting politely. She liked Nicos. And although she had never consciously spoken about him to anyone, she felt an attraction, which she hoped was reciprocated, or might be one day. As their professional lives criss-crossed often, it meant they saw a lot of each other.

"I hear you found the boy." Nicos said as an opener then waited for her to finish the coffee.

"Yes, well, what is left of him? Come, I will show you."

"Sure." Nicos got up from the chair, waited for her, and together walked the short distance to the morgue.

"I hear a tourist disappeared too, have you found him yet?" Elena asked.

"No, not yet, we are still looking. The boats and the coastguard are out now, and we will start a helicopter search first thing tomorrow. But I think the chances of finding him are slim. I thought it might be murder, three friends killing a friend, but no, two tourists followed his friends up the stairs and had their video camera on, shot a panoramic view, even got the guy standing on the rocks before he jumped. So that lets them off the hook. Can't be in two places at once, can they?"

"You know, for a police officer, I think you watch too much CSI." She smiled.

Nicos waited for Elena to open the door then pushed it further ajar as it was stiff. The room was clean, with a distinct chemical aroma of blended bleach and ammonia permeating the air.

"He's over here. It's not pretty." Elena guided Nicos towards the steel trolley. "I haven't even started the examination yet, just looked him over and took a few shots. See for yourself."

Like Elena, Nicos had seen death in all its guises, but not like this. The horror that revealed itself could have come from the makeup department of a movie production, only this scene was very real. Nicos took an involuntary step backwards. The body was also beginning to smell, and the noxious odour cut into the senses of the two people in the room.

Elena daubed a small amount of perfume from her tanned handbag on a tissue and gave it to Nicos then repeated the procedure for herself.

He took the tissue, nodded his thanks, and moved closer to the body. Leaning in, he noticed that at the bottom of one of the deeper wounds there appeared to be a small sharp object protruding from just inside the wound. "May I?" Holding of a pair of small tweezers, he dipped it into the wound, pinched the object, and held it gently between the pincers. Then taking a small plastic bag from his pocket, he opened it, and dropped the sharp object into it. "I will take it for analysis, as it shouldn't make a difference to your examination." He smiled.

"No. But if it does, I will let you know. Well, I think I'd better start and see what we can find out about how this poor boy died. Maybe I'll see you later?"

"Yes, call me, and we can meet for a drink if you like." Nicos kissed her as he had done before but thought about a more passionate kiss. But not in this setting. He smiled, winked, pushed the door open, and was back in the corridor.

Now, alone in the room, Elena moved to the trestle table in front of her and studied the array of instruments that adorned it. Picking up a piece of note paper, she wrote the name down. Nilu Comaneci, aged nine. Next to the name she placed a question mark and a number 7872700. "Where to begin?" she said aloud, as if the occupants in the room were listening to her every word.

Nicosia, Monday, 6am

The harsh shriek of the early morning cockerel broke the silence of the new day. Spyro stared at the bedside table clock, it had stopped at three-thirty, so the alarm had not gone off. He was sure he had checked the batteries, so it should have been alright, but the only bell ringing now was the one in his head telling him he was late, an occurrence that had happened only once before in thirty-five years. He climbed quickly out of bed and dressed, pulling socks, shoes, and shorts on in one swift movement. A slightly grimy vest was next as he moved rapidly to his ablutions in the bathroom.

Nicos had called his friend Alexis Stavides, who was a former classmate and now a respected marine biologist, who had just returned from a visit to Mauritius. He had rung him late, to check if they could meet, but the earliest Alexis could manage was six the next morning, as he was an early riser. Nicos agreed, and left his apartment in Strovolos to drive the short distance to the house and lab in Akaki Palaiometocho on the B9.

The road was usually quite fast and there shouldn't be too much morning traffic, especially for Nicos' BMW 6 series. His one major luxury. Yes, his apartment was comfortable, but not luxurious, but his car, that was a different matter. He almost felt as if he could live in it, a type of home away from home, even though the bank owned it. Like a lot of Cypriots, who want to buy something, they must go to the bank to do so. However, in these harsh days of austerity, the banks rarely loaned to anyone unless they had a concrete agreement that the debt could be paid. Fortunately for Nicos, he had got in early, so he got his loan.

His only other concession to his lifestyle, was the colour white. After all, he was a police officer, and the idea of a bright blue ΑΣΤΥΝΟΜΙΑ emblazoned on the front of his bonnet just did not appeal. So, for the purpose of driving, he stayed incognito.

Picking up the small plastic bag with the sample inside, he placed it on the dashboard by the instrument panel, and drove down towards the end of his street to join with the main Strovolos road. Straddling the Nicosia Mall and GSP Stadium, it's where the Cypriot international football team play most of their games and where Champion's League matches are also played. Something which in recent years has seen the Cypriot teams of Apoel and Ael challenge the big boys.

Noticing the traffic was building up as the early rush hour car queues began to form, he drove into the outside lane and accelerated past two labouring lorries, as they made their way into the capital, Nicosia.

In Orounta, Spyro drank a cold glass of water and picked up his cell phone. There was no signal. Abandoning the idea of letting someone know he might be late, he climbed into the lorry's cab and started the engine; it punched in loudly and he reversed out into the narrow road, avoiding the few chickens that had come to peck and scavenge.

He drove slowly up the lane and past the large imposing Orthodox Church. A short, old widow dressed all in black sat on the bench outside. He nodded to her as he accelerated past, turned into the slip-road that led to the main artery, and noticed how the village seemed unusually quiet. He glanced at his watch and thought there should be more people milling about, even at this time of morning. Then returning his attention to the driving, he filtered into the main road, put his foot down, and worked to make up lost time as he watched the speedometer rise.

Passing two cars in quick succession, Nicos gunned the accelerator. This was a fast road but could also be a dangerous one; many a young driver had been killed on this stretch over the years. It was also a road that took him close to the infamous green line, the marker that separated the Greek part of Cyprus from the occupied North where the Turks had taken up residence since their invasion of 1974. Nowhere was this more noticeable on this section of road than at the once bustling airport of Nicosia, now slap bang in the middle of no-man's land.

Due to his age, he had never known the island other than how it was, yet his parents, who were once landowners in Famagusta, were among the thousands of refugees who had fled south to avoid the Turks. His father had died young, in his early forties, but his mother was still alive and lived with Nicos' sister in Omodos, the region famous for its majestic wines. He tried to visit them on weekends but work usually kept him busy so he couldn't always make it, but as a dutiful son, he managed to keep in touch.

Spyros's lorry had passed the familiar aroma of the pig-pens. This was the centre for 'bringing home the bacon'. Most of the villages in this region, and all around the area, were noted for its pig industry on the island. After a while, the stench becomes second nature to those who live there but for the tourist or visitor, it could be a shock to the system, especially the nostrils.

He stepped down hard on the throttle and the engine roared as the heavy ten-ton lorry bustled its way down the road. As he came to the main traffic junction, he began to signal right. A small moped pushed its way in front of him and he slammed on his brakes. The swearing inside the cab was audible from the outside, which was mostly made up of one word "malacca", said repeatedly. Still gesticulating at the moped driver, he turned the wheel to join the B9.

The BMW was traveling at a good speed and Nicos quickly checked his watch, as the car glided effortlessly away. How he wished he had one of those stick-on lights they used on cop car shows. He imitated the sound to himself, then thought better of it as he slowed for a set of traffic lights.

As he sat waiting for the lights to change, he noticed the small object inside the plastic bag had begun to glow. He checked again, it wasn't the sun's reflection and as he watched, the glimmer became brighter, turning to an almost vivid orange. The lights at the junction changed from amber to red.

Inside the lorry, the temperature was starting to rise as Spyro went through the gears and the sun grew brighter. To protect his eyes, he pulled the sun visor down. He almost slammed his brakes on, because right there was the picture of his wife, Maria. The picture he usually kept in his wallet. *"How did it get here?"* he mused.

Confused and a little shocked, he reached inside his shorts to pull out the wallet, while staring at the picture. It became a scramble inside his pocket as the wallet had lodged itself and was stuck. Unable to reach the bulky object as the seatbelt restricted his movements, he undid the strap and tried to pull it free, while trying to keep one eye on the road, and the other hand on the wheel. He located the wallet and began to fumble inside; the picture was not there. He was sure he had not taken it out. But there it was, on the visor.

As Nicos moved away from the lights, the radiance inside the car was now becoming brighter with each passing yard. He stretched his hand across to take the item from the plastic bag, and as he touched it, he felt a searing sting as the object's sharp edge punctured one fingertip. He winced as an incredible smarting pain shot through him and blood dribbled onto the pristine dashboard. Swiftly, he pushed the bleeding digit into his mouth and tried to suck the cut, as he busied himself looking for a tissue to stem the flow.

Anxious to put the picture back in his wallet, Spyro reached across. He tried to grab it but somehow it stayed out of reach, as if it was in some way teasing him. He leaned further and his other hand lost control of the wheel.

The lorry careered across the road out of control, the wheels spun and the tyres screeched, and smoke billowed from the brakes as he slammed against the kerb trying to avoid the white BMW headed straight towards him.

It was the first time Nicos and Spyro met, and it was their last.

The lorry raced towards the small car and Nicos watched helplessly as the monster edged closer and closer. Then, it hit the driver's side; the airbag inside the BMW activated but for some inexplicable reason did not inflate.

Nicos felt the agony of metal on flesh as the engine mounts snapped and the huge diesel engine slid straight into his car, crushing everything in its path until it smashed through the steering column and impaled his body as the raw steel speared him to his seat.

The noise created an overture to disaster, metal grinding and glass smashing, a muffled scream and a final deafening explosion as both petrol tanks ignited from the spilled petroleum that now flooded across the road.

All other traffic stopped and became reluctant witnesses to the scene unfolding before them.

In their last little vignettes of life, Spyro tried to stretch across to pick up the picture, the one that had tormented him, the one that had teased him, and the one that had killed him. His eyes closing as Maria's face became the only light he saw.

Flames ignited upholstery and the choking thick cloud snaked its way inside the vehicle. The once smart white upholstery had now turned grey as the smoke funnelled and slowly suffocated Nicos.

But he couldn't move his legs, for what was left of them was smashed into sticks of bone. The agony and pain and suffering he was experiencing was only amplified by the beating and thrashing of his heart as it fought for life. As the fire gripped the vehicle, the first sirens began to wail down the road. His heart slowed, its vibrations stopped, and he gripped the piece of steel protruding from his body as the inferno took hold and raged through to the interior of the BMW, incinerating everything inside.

Death can be quick in Cyprus.

Frimley, Monday, 5pm

Sitting quietly on the sofa, Richard waited for Julie to return. She had reacted badly to his phone call from Peter. So much so that it had led to another argument, another angry outburst, then the silence, and she had stormed out of the room; her usual reaction to something she didn't like. It was her way of assessing the situation. As he waited, the voice in his head continued tormenting him.

"I am waiting, Richard, don't let me down." The goddess's voice became a parasite to his thoughts.

Now, resolved to the situation, Julie came back into the room. She had cried openly but had managed to compose herself. She sat opposite her husband and looked at him, she wanted answers. But the one burning question she wanted answered was also the most difficult to ask. She asked it anyway. "Does this thing have anything to do with Aphrodite's Rock?" She stared at him, her eyes already questioning his response.

"No, not directly, except that it is about the money involved when I was there. As I said, they are taking Peter to court as he is the one over there and they are holding him responsible for the debt."

"Is that all it is, nothing else?"

He stayed calm. She had not asked what he knew she wanted to, *'what has this got to do with the goddess?'* That was the real question, but for some reason, she decided to stay away from it.

"Jules, if there was a way to get around this without going, I would grab it. I have offered to Skype them, but they won't accept it. I have to appear in person, I have to go to Cyprus, and Peter needs my help."

"How long will it take?" She seemed resigned to the idea.

"I will be back in a few days, no more than a week, at most. But you know how slow the wheels turn there."

"They didn't turn that slow last time you needed something." Her quick reminder of his last meeting with bureaucracy was something she had not forgotten.

"Maybe I can see Mr Christoulides again, perhaps he can sort this out."

"Seems like a plan, I suggest you ring him."

"I will as soon as I get there. I will also start looking for flights now. Apparently, the court date is Friday. I will meet Peter in Paphos and then we can sort it out."

"Was Peter okay? How is he coping without Sheila? That was such a shock, finding out they had split."

"He seemed okay. Says the house hasn't sold yet, but he's staying at a friend's place in Paphos, flat sitting. Says there is enough room for me, so I don't need to find an apartment and that will save some money. Just find a cheap flight on Easy Jet or Ryan Air, or perhaps one of the charters. I'll be fine, I won't take a lot with me."

"Do you want me to come?"

Her question was unexpected as she had often reiterated, she would never return.

"Do you want to?" Richard had to play this cagey; put the onus back on her. "Are you okay with that?"

"Not really, I never want to go back there. But if you need me, I will."

"I tell you what. I'll go over and see what the situation is. Then if I need you, I'll call so you can come over. Is that fair?"

"Yes, that's okay with me." Julie leaned over and kissed her husband lightly on the lips. She loved him and he loved her, of that she was certain.

It was enough to keep them together. But with the weight of guilt pressing upon him and what he was expected to do, he had already begun to doubt it.

CHAPTER FOUR

A Reckoning

The B9 was closed for most of the day as the crime and forensic team got to work sifting through the grisly remains of the two charred vehicles. The fire had been so intense that Nicos' body was burnt beyond recognition and only the most hardened of police and firemen were able to do what needed to be done, and the fact that it was one of their own made the task all the more difficult. Whatever Nicos was working on went to the grave with him. His notes were almost always cryptic, and it was practically impossible to unravel the words he had scribbled together. The only definite evidence he had taken lately was the statement he had from the young Englishman at Protaras station, and that was in no way linked to this tragedy.

It would be a little longer than usual but both funerals would take place in the next few days; the village of Orounta would turn out once more for Spyro, and the City of Nicosia would salute one of its finest.

Meanwhile, Barry's body had drifted for four days; his torso ripped to pieces by forces unknown. What remained was more like a stump of flesh that bobbled up and down in the water. As night fell, several container and passenger ships ferried their way between Larnaca and Limassol on the busy shipping lanes of the two ports.

Cyprus is involved in an expansive maritime plan with marinas being agreed upon and developed across most of the main ports of the island. Larnaca, Paphos, and Ayia Napa were all in the pipeline, but Limassol was the latest to open, raising the prestige of the city, and encouraging people to buy property in and around the quay developments with prices ranging from four hundred and fifty thousand to a few million Euros. Marinas were big business.

Out at sea and in the darkness, one container ship moving slowly through the water looked much like any other and as the vessels grew closer to their destination, the activity on board began to escalate above and below decks, so it was all too easy to miss a piece of flotsam idly bobbing gently up and down in the waves.

As Barry's body drifted into the sea lanes, it moved into the path of the one of the containers heading towards port. The ship's engines now placed in reverse to slow it down, made the waters around the huge propellers churn, whipping up water around the metal fans and stirring the waves like a giant ladle. The suction created a vortex, just like a bath-plug being pulled and the contents emptied, only, instead of the foaming bubbles of 'Radox' what was going down this particular hole was the last remnants of Barry Rochester, as what was left of his body struck the metal propeller and became mince for the fish.

The ship moved on through the darkness.

CHAPTER FIVE

The Zenobia

Larnaca Offshore, Tuesday

Sun Divers had been operating in Cyprus for the past eight years, and in all that time, they had put hundreds of people through PADI diving courses. But the recession had bitten Sun Divers hard and whereas they used to make three or four trips out to the wrecks off the coast, they now just made one a week. And that was to the MS Zenobia; the roll-on-roll-off Swedish cargo ferry that had capsized on its maiden voyage on the third of June 1980, with a full complement of cargo. Fortunately, all the crew got off safely and there were no casualties, but as the ship listed and salvage became impossible, the MS Zenobia sank into the waters off Larnaca on June 7th at 2:30am to take up its permanent position at 34'53.5" N, 33'39.1" to become one of the world's most spectacular wrecks, still with its two hundred million pounds' worth of cargo on board.

For Lenny Speagel and his wife, Jenny, the MS Zenobia had become a bit like a second home. Both knew the vessel well, treated it with the greatest respect, and often reminded themselves of its track record of four diving deaths. Whilst most areas of the ship are safe and accessible, other parts can be deadly, as it is all too easy to get lost. Once that happens, the chances of finding your way back before the oxygen runs out are remote. Fortunately, none of the divers at Sun Divers had ever been in that position. Lenny liked to keep a tight ship.

As the boat made its way out from Larnaca, the six men and women began to kit-up with last-minute adjustments in preparation for their dive. Jenny was pleased with the group because they had all dived the wreck before, which meant that she too could go down, and not babysit this time.

The sea around the wreck was calm as the boat came to a gradual stop then dropped anchor. The first two divers leaned against the side of the hull and disappeared backwards, over, and under the water. The small bubbles that surfaced showed their equipment working well.

Jenny put her mask on and waited for Lenny, as he tied a rope around the remaining air tanks and together, they joined the others in the crystal blue ocean. Dressed in wetsuits, it was difficult to gauge temperature and the water's glass-like clarity created the impression of coolness as they filed past a few fish stragglers. As they swam deeper, silt and sand billowed towards them. What was causing it neither was sure.

The Zenobia was, at forty-two metres, lying on its side on the seabed. Some of its cargo, including a few of the hundred plus lorries, scattered over the bottom. To the rear of the vessel, more spilled cargo littered the floor, including pots of paint, rusting air conditioners, and some Tonka Toys, which made the scene even more surreal.

Jenny looked around to see some of the group entering the wreck and motioned to Lenny that she was following them. His raised thumb indicated his approval and he moved away towards the bow. Once inside, she began to explore, her air bubbles the only audible sound as she scooted in and out of the deck. Even now and after all these years of diving, she sometimes still discovered new things that she had not seen before, for as she moved down the ship gangway, she spotted a shiny object. It was a small silver coin, possibly a Swedish Kroner that had wedged itself into a grating on the deck. She placed it inside a small pocket on her wetsuit before moving back along her chosen course.

Just ahead, something caught her attention; something else was moving. She wasn't sure what it was, but it looked black in colour and had a distinct side to side movement. As she drew nearer, she reached for her small waterproof torch; it would give her just enough light to check it out.

As the shape moved away from her, Jenny followed cautiously, and checked her watch; she had about ten minutes of air left and should turn back, but this was somehow exciting as she followed the unfamiliar shape.

Moving stealthily along the decks, visibility decreased rapidly, and it became difficult to see what undulated and slithered ahead of her. The feelings that crept through her were no longer that of excitement, but anxiety, and dread that something might be lying in wait for her. It made no sense to go on, especially as she could not see two feet in front of her nose, but she quickly put those fears aside and continued the chase.

What became instantly obvious was the intense stillness. All wrecks creak, and occasionally rattle, the MS Zenobia was no different. But today she was silent, and with each move Jenny took, she felt herself being drawn further away from where she needed to be. As she moved slowly, cautiously, she hoped Lenny was already looking for her. She clicked the torch on, and the beam lit the floor below her. How far she had gone down she wasn't sure, as she was not familiar with this part of the ship.

A few more strokes with her gloved hands and an open door appeared before her, with just enough room to squeeze through. This was new, somewhere she had never been before and had to push hard against the metal to open it. With her torch piercing through the darkness, she scanned the surrounding area, and felt a surge of water enter the room, followed by a much larger gushing sound as the floor began to open below her. Looking down and through the half-light, two large bright red eyes moved towards her, slowly then at a rapid speed, faster and faster they came at her. Frozen by fear, she only managed to stare back at them, then she turned, and banged on the door.

She dropped her torch, its beam shining down into the hole, and the sudden bright light distracted whatever it was that was coming for her. She turned, again trying to get away. Pushing herself through the door as fast as she could, she felt her legs freeze and her body shake, it was all she could do to stop herself from urinating in her wet suit, the terror too real, as whatever it was, moved back into its sanctuary. Fighting for every breath, she struggled to find the exit. The air now very low in her tank, she saw daylight, or what she thought was, and left the wreck, pushing out her arms and legs in a frantic motion, and began swimming straight for the surface.

Lenny was still below the water looking for her when he spotted her swimming to the surface. He came up at once and swam quickly to his wife, holding her as she ripped the mask from her face. Tears streaming down her face, she shook visibly in the water as if wrapped in ice. He didn't say anything, just eased her closer to the edge as two of the men on the boat leaned forward to drag her on board.

CHAPTER SIX

Expect the unexpected

Larnaca, Oroklini, Tuesday, 10:30pm
In the living room of the Speagel's, two empty brandy glasses glistened in the half-glow of the lounge lights. Lenny stood up and came across to his wife, who was lying on the couch, her face pale, as she lay dead still. She had been like this for almost half an hour. The only time she moved from her place was to sink the brandy.

He tried comforting her, stroking her hair, holding one of her hands, and cradling her to him. "It's alright. You are fine now. I got you."

Of course, he was trying to make her feel safe, but she didn't feel safe at all.

"Do you think you can tell me what happened down there? You haven't said a word all the way back in the boat, or in the car, everyone is worried. What happened to you?"

As if recalling in a flash what happened, she sat bolt upright. "Lenny, you must never go there again, never, do you hear me? Never."

"We can't do that, love, there are no other dive sites we can use, and this is the only thing we have left. If we stop going, someone else will take our place. We won't have any money coming in, we will be bankrupt, and lose everything. You know how bad things have been."

"I don't care. Promise me, Lenny, just promise me." Her eyes filled with tears as she began to shake, the feelings she had felt in the water now returned. She closed her eyes for a second and saw again the menacing red pair that looked back at her on the ship. She opened hers again, tears streaming down her face. "Promise me, Lenny, please."

He held her closer. He knew he had to make the promise, but in all honesty, didn't know how to. And if he agreed about not returning, then the life they knew was over. If that was to happen, whatever was in those depths had already claimed another victim.

Frimley, Tuesday, 10:30pm

It was Richard's last night before he left for Cyprus. His last night with Julie, and maybe, his last forever. It was a cruel thought probing his mind as he readied himself for bed and his marital duty.

Up until today, he had never thought of love-making as a duty, but in this instance, it seemed to fit, even if what he was really doing was following orders; those of a being not of this world, one that tormented and tortured him relentlessly. It was this more than any other thought that made him think of his last night with Julie as a duty; perhaps once a soldier, always a soldier.

Whatever was to happen on this night one thing was sure, he must put the goddess out of his head. It was Julie only now. Only she mattered. He loved her and wanted her as he always had, but this time must be special, so special, he could not let anything, or anyone spoil it.

As he walked into their bedroom, the bedside light on the small table was on, and Julie sat reading a book.

She had her glasses on but as she became aware of him, she looked over them, smiled, and pulled the sheet slowly back. She was wearing just her bra, which was soon disposed of as she reached behind and snapped off the hook, before slowly and seductively letting it fall from her breasts.

Moving across to her, he took her in his arms pressing himself tight against her. His way of saying, "I won't ever let go."

She hugged him, then lay back to allow him the pleasure of her body.

He leaned in and kissed her passionately, before sliding down her naked body, his hands moving slowly and sensuously across her. He kept staring at her and then leaning down to kiss her repeatedly, closing his eyes tight, as if he knew when he opened them, she would be gone. She returned his kisses while moving with him as he probed and stroked. He ran his hands lightly over her, one palm pushing against her lower stomach with the heel of his hand, and his fingers deftly began searching out her contours. She began to move under him, and her breathing became erratic as he began to explore her.

He opened his eyes as her body writhed and wriggled across the sheets as he entered her and began to make love to her. This was love-making, intense, pure, and honest; not fucking, and there was no lust, just a complete feeling of togetherness as they enjoyed each other.

"Love me." His words drifted on the pillow as he felt his whole body begin to throb.

Julie held him tight as he felt her own body tighten and climax in his arms.

He had completed his duty, then he lay back still repeating to himself, "love me, love me."

"I do, Richard, and soon you will find out just how much." The goddess' words echoed in his head.

'Not now.' He thought. *'Not now.'* And a small tear rolled from his right eye to nestle on the pillow.

If Julie saw it or not, he wasn't sure, as he leaned over quickly to turn off the bedside table light. Before he returned to holding her close, but even as he did, he couldn't be sure it was her.

CHAPTER SEVEN

Aftermath

Oroklini, Wednesday
That morning, Lenny set off early, leaving his wife sleeping; the sedative he had given her not simply a means to relax but also to make certain she slept longer than usual. This would help him with the plan he had hastily concocted. From first-light, he had been assembling all the gear he figured he would need and walked around the house bare-feet, tiptoeing past the bedroom door when he needed something. By 7:30am, he was ready.

He started the truck and made sure the equipment stored in the back was secure. The small vile of liquid rested inside a larger case and he moved it delicately to a spot among the gear, tying it with a thick red cord to make certain it did not move. To cover everything, he threw a tarpaulin over, keeping it hidden from prying eyes on the drive to the boat, which would take about half an hour if the traffic was okay.

It was just after 8:20am when he next checked his watch. It was later than he thought, but that hardly mattered. He took the boat, started the engine, and made his way from the quay where he habitually moored out to the open sea. The sun was already warm, as its rays coated his shoulders. The boat moved through the gears as it picked up speed, heading out to the Zenobia wreck.

The sea was calm as he steered the craft almost nonchalantly and poured himself a small cup of coffee from a flask, and just for good measure, added a wee dram to the cup and drank it swiftly. Normally, he didn't drink, especially not at this time of day, and certainly not Scotch, but today he felt he needed some extra Dutch courage for he had no idea who, or what, he was looking for.

He stopped the boat as he approached the dive site, collected all his gear together, and reached for the long case. He took out the small vile and carefully opened it, pouring a small drop of its contents into a small beaker and returned it to its resting place. He opened the canvas hold-all behind him, took out the short spear gun, and dipped one of the tips into the liquid. While replacing the red cap on the tip of the spear, the faintest droplet of liquid rolled down the shaft, but he ignored it, instead, getting into his diving suit quickly, he attached the weapon and heavy-duty torch to his belt, and lowered himself over the side. His oxygen tank was half full; he hoped it was enough for what he needed.

The water was clear as he descended. In fact, having a better clarity than the previous day, no silt coming up from the seabed and as he took out his torch and shone it down, the reflections of a lorry's bonnet bounced back towards the beam. Swimming slowly, he eased his way towards the wreck, noticing as he did that the usual collection of fish and crabs seemed fewer than normal. As he approached them, they became skittish; the fish swam away, and the crabs ran for cover. He too felt uneasy, sensing a presence, and moved to take the spear gun from the side of his belt. Holding it in his hand, and with the torch in the other, he landed on the seabed. The silence was extreme as he stood there, just the rhythm of his oxygen bubbles permeating the serene sea.

Why did he feel so wary and more than a little scared? It was as if fear itself was transmitting from the wreck, like a prelude to disaster, feeling almost tangible, and its scream deafening. He shone the beam from bow to stern like a searchlight, skimming across the ship; nothing.

He knew he had to go inside, so he flicked at the red tip on the top of the spear, and moved forward, the lethal poison now ready to be used against whatever was on that ship. His movement across the floor kicked up sand, decreasing visibility and he decided that swimming would be a better choice as he pushed towards the hull. He checked his watch, there were about fifteen minutes of oxygen left, which seemed to have gone much quicker than expected.

He looked around again, nothing; but as he moved forward, he caught a glimpse of a dark fleeting form moving across the hull and away from him. Pushing the torch into his belt, he swam towards the shape, his heart and lungs beating harder and faster with the increasing pressure of the chase. He pivoted quickly as the figure changed direction with him in pursuit, his adrenaline pumping as fast as his heart was, and felt exhilarated as he gave whatever it was the best hunt of its life.

As he drew closer, he could see what looked like scales on the back of an indistinct contour. His excitement now mixed, it also took over, as he swam harder and faster as determination pushed him to the limit to find this thing. But just as he reached one of the rotting overturned lorries, his body suddenly jerked and he felt a numbness enter as an excruciating pain shot through him. As muscle and sinew ripped from his arm, flooding the floor below in vibrant spatters of red, his blood jetted out in one thin stream and flowed from the gaping wound that opened wider as the richer thicker blood spurted from his slashed arteries, spilling out onto the sand. In seconds, he began to lose consciousness, almost instantly his face drained, and a white ghostly pallor appeared under his mask.

Just barely alive, he tried to reach for the spear gun with his other arm, but the second attack gave him no chance of reply, as his stomach shredded open. His agony unimaginable and the sound of the attack beyond vicious, the noise of his torn flesh and tattered wetsuit splitting in two echoed across the junkyard of the seabed.

Whatever protection the suit gave him became null and void against the frenzied assault as his scattered flesh joined the human offal of internal organs that dribbled from his body and coated what was left of the suit, before being deposited at his feet on the floor. Lenny's last act of defiance was to open his eyes to see his killer; he had his answer, as they shut forever.

Frimley, 8am

His plane didn't leave until 2pm but Richard couldn't sleep. He had tossed and turned and gone back and forth during the night to hold Julie, then let go again as he rolled onto his side. Not since her last words, had he heard anymore from the goddess. It seemed she sensed he was coming and could manipulate him at will. He, on the other hand, never knew when and what to expect from her.

As he sat in the back garden, the morning sun flickered through the trees at the back of the house. He stared for a few seconds at the empty garden and recalled the voices of his kids as they were growing up. He could see the first tentative tries from Matthew as he made his way up and down on his little red second-hand bike and watched as Molly pushed her toy pram back and forth, her dolls and teddies spilling over onto the freshly cut lawn. It seemed a long time ago but those memories were locked in that garden; he just had to open his mind to see them, and did.

He sipped his coffee but was unable to hide or disguise the feelings that riddled him with guilt. He should tell Julie the truth, be honest with her, but he also knew that if he did, he would be putting his whole family, not just her, in jeopardy, and that he could not do. He had to go, for that was the right thing to do. The only thing to do.

Nicosia District, 10am

Black enveloped the village of Orounta; the people wore black, the cars were all draped in black, and above the village, as if in simpatico, a small dark cloud made its way over the congregation, breaking into the sunlight that had begun to lose its lustre. As the congregation filed into the red brick Orthodox Church, the tolling of a single bell echoed down through the streets and houses, and that same cloud moved effortlessly towards Nicosia, where another congregation gathered; they too were all dressed in black.

The funerals of Spyro and Nicos had both made the news. Huddled together and away from the main mourners, two small groups of reporters and newsmen gathered, busily taking notes, and recording images.

In both locations, Orounta and Nicosia, the grief was the same, as together they mourned the loss of their sons. But for one young woman, the heartache was even greater. For she grieved, not for what she had lost but for what she might have had. Elena's soft white handkerchief was stained with her mascara, her tears, and she wept openly on the steps of Ayia Paraskevi Church.

Limassol, later the same day
The meeting was called almost immediately after the funerals. It would be held away from the city at Governor's Beach, in the beachside conference centre 'The Thallassa', as the fish menus were particularly good at the restaurant, so they would also make a night of it.

The main delegates for the meeting were from the principal cities and municipalities, those who had vested interests in maritime affairs, in particular, the marinas. Seated around the table in a quiet corner of the restaurant were Panayotis Linos, Christina Skalos, Francoise Mulot, and Gregor Tabachi; the four held a good deal of power and influence, particularly in matters of finance and investment.

"A sad day…" Panayotis was first to speak as he lifted his glass of chilled white Frascati. "I didn't know the officer personally, I mean, Inspector, but I hear he was very good at his job."

"Yes, a sad day." Gregor picked up a small bread roll from the basket on the table and began to tear it open. He took a large dollop of butter and placed it on his knife before spreading it lavishly. "We are here to decide what we should do about these incidents, yes?" His Russian accent becoming more pronounced with each word uttered.

"Personally, I think we should just ignore them." The Parisian lilt of Francoise's voice interrupted Gregor's flow as she too collected a bread roll.

"It's easy to ignore, yes." Panayotis' words tried to hold a balance as he began to pour yet another glass of Frascati. "But I think we need to look at the facts. To date, we have had two bodies go missing in the past ten days, and one of them was found in a terrible state, the other... well, God knows where it is. And no one has a clue what happened to them. There is even talk of a Cryptid claiming them."

"What is a Cryptid?" Francoise was first to ask, but everyone wanted the same answer.

"You have not heard of it? This is the term given to sea monsters. It is said one inhabits the coast around Ayia Napa and Cape Greco..." Panayotis was beginning to enjoy holding court but stopped short as the waiters brought their fish to the table.

All had chosen the dish of the day, Sea Bass with prawns and limes, plus various shellfish as a side dish, complimented by a rich Greek salad crested with lumps of Feta.

Panayotis picked up his knife and fork and began to cut into his fish, before speaking again. "The locals call it 'Filiko Teras' which translates as 'The Friendly Monster'. It's a Cypriot myth, been around for years."

"Well, myth or not, we can't afford any more bad publicity. Not with all the problems we have with the bailout and finding investors. The money tied up with these marinas is huge and we all know what it can do for the country; it could become our economy's life saver, at least in the short-term." Christina was very vocal as she began to dig into her fish with her knife.

"Christina is right, there is too much at stake, we have to handle this carefully. Any hint of ridicule with this monster idea and investors may shy away from the plans." Gregor's Russian stoical approach underlined his comment.

"Personally, I think it has a certain appeal. A friendly monster could be a big tourist attraction as well. Look at what has happened to Aphrodite's Rocks since last year. More popular than ever, so a monster tale could be a great marketing tool for us, if handled correctly." Francoise's thinking was now in marketing overdrive.

"Yes, but I am not so sure where deaths are involved. I think we need to stay quiet and stick with the drowning story for the time being it has probably been the most sensible so far. People will believe that more readily than any monster nonsense." Panayotis cut the head off his fish and placed it on the side of his plate.

"I still think it would be a good attraction. Look at Loch Ness, they have no evidence. Well, no real evidence, yet they made a complete industry out of their monster." Francoise reclined in her chair, she had finished her fish and her mind was no longer on the meal.

Gregor folded his knife and fork over the plate, his fish now disembodied, a lean piece of skin and discarded bones decorating his plate. He bent forward. "My people have millions tied up in these plans, I am not going back to them with tales of monsters or any such shit. The explanation will be that the kid and the tourist, if they ever find him, drowned. It is unfortunate but a fact and the reason the boy's body was so badly disfigured was because he was dragged under a boat and the propellers cut through him. That is enough."

"May I add one more caveat to that?" Francoise leaned across the table, her eyes wide as she looked at each of her compatriots, examining them, looking for a reaction as she spoke. "What if there is another body that goes missing, or is washed up on a tourist beach somewhere? What do we say to our people then?"

The question posed many more questions, ones that could not be answered right away. But it meant only one thing, they had to see what happened next and if there would be another body discovered.

CHAPTER EIGHT

Back to Cyprus

Gatwick Airport, midday

Knowing the airline wouldn't serve any meals, Julie made a packed lunch; put together a ham and chicken sandwich, also included an apple, and a chocolate bar, Dairy Milk, his favourite. It was these little things that he cherished most about her, how she always looked out for him, how without even thinking about it, she could show her love in the smallest of gestures. He adored her for that. This was something he knew the goddess would never understand.

He leaned back in the plane seat and closed his eyes, his text to Peter mere confirmation that he would pick him up as he waited to taxi down the runway, while avoiding Felicity's eyes, one of the air crew.

As far as he could tell, Julie did not suspect a thing. He held her close and kissed her gently before he set off through immigration control and into the departure lounge.

She merely spoke one sentence. "Let me know you're okay, okay?"

Would he ever be okay again? His life was about to change again, and he seemed powerless to do much about it, controlled by a malevolent spirit that just wouldn't take no for an answer.

Sitting in the aircraft, he again wondered how he had done this to himself. How did he make her become real, or was it just his imagination, furtive as it was? Had the PTSD finally kicked in and he was now heading down the long road to total insanity? If anything, it would make more sense than what he was facing. Was his psychopathic creation a figment of his imagination or a symptom of his delayed illness?

"No, Richard, I am real."

Great, she was reading his thoughts.

Paphos, 6pm

Sitting, drinking his coffee, and scanning the web pages for arrivals to check if the plane was on time, Peter again looked at his watch, knowing it wouldn't take him more than twenty-five minutes to get to the airport. Besides, sometimes the delays at baggage collection added another twenty to thirty minutes before clearing into the arrivals hall. If Richard got through okay and wasn't too long or too knackered, maybe they could get a quick couple of games of pool and he could find out what this was all about.

For Richard, the plane was on time, and there were no delays. A slight smile spread over his lips as the aircraft touched down on the runway at Paphos, and it was greeted by the somewhat odd custom of applause from inside the cabin.

Outside, the evening airport lights twinkled against a bright night sky, which was full of stars. The crew emptied out of their seats, followed by one or two impatient passengers, who were instantly told, "to sit down until the aircraft has come to a complete stop".

Richard peered out of the window. He couldn't help it, it felt as if he were arriving home. That, was a dangerous thought.

Setting off from his apartment, Peter took it easy. The traffic down the Tomb of The King's Road was relatively light, but it was going slower than usual; probably because of the neat little police speed-trap tucked away in one of the bus stop lay-bys. Fortunately, the unwritten law of flashing headlights from the opposite direction when the police were near was always a good warning signal to motorists. It is one of the few courtesies some Cypriot drivers accord their fellow road users.

Following his fellow passengers down the stairs, Richard made his way into the immigration line for EEC travellers, which were spelt out in big yellow letters suspended over the top of one of the booths, and twinned with the bright yellow line painted on the floor that made sure no one crossed it before they were intended to.

The line was not particularly long as he had got through the impatient throng quite quickly by dodging the push and wheelchairs, all uniformly lined up waiting to be escorted through. He took out his passport and looked around. There were just a couple of people in uniforms walking around, a girl, no more than early twenties, with a neat bun hairstyle and little makeup. Next to her, was a much older man, slightly portly, who seemed to be the one in charge, as he watched and inspected the visitors arriving into his homeland.

Richard was next in line. He looked across at the immigration girl with the bun and smiled.

She looked back at him and didn't, but it was clear she recognised him.

He moved up to the booth, crossing the yellow line, and spoke in his best Greek. "Yasso."

The man in the booth said nothing, but took his passport, placed it on the desk, and flicked through the pages. He glanced up for a second and pressed a couple of keys on the keyboard. The screen opened and a string of words blanketed the page. He didn't look at Richard as he moved to take a large photo album from beside him and flicked through the pages.

"Wait here." His English was good enough to be understood.

The queue behind Richard began to build and people's faces showed their frustration.

The portly man came across to Richard, flanked by the young girl, and the man from the booth. "Follow me, please."

They took him away from the queue and out into a small corridor. Nobody said anything, their steps words enough as they made their way towards a small interview room.

"Wait here."

He was ushered inside.

The girl followed him in and stood at the opposite wall as he took his seat.

He sat on the wooden chair and began to pick his fingers, always a sign that his nerves were jangling. He looked at the girl, and again she said nothing. He didn't speak either, but knew she recognised him.

The door opened and the portly man returned, "Follow me, please."

Richard hoped his English extended to more than wait and follow but like the good lap dog that he was, he duly followed.

The portly man opened another door that said, 'No Admittance'.

Richard pre-empted the comment. "Wait here."

The portly man said nothing.

As far as he could judge, he was standing inside a large hangar, bright plane lights shimmering as he looked around him, and outside, he could hear the roar of aircraft engines.

"Mr Cole, is it?" A short man spoke the question.

An imposing man, one who was impeccably dressed in a serge blue suit, stunning black shoes that seemed to have a light all their own because they sparkled so much, and with his crowning glory, a sharp crisp white shirt open at the neck. His face was ruddy and well-groomed, that's to say, his beard was trimmed to absolute perfection, not a hair out-of-place, and his eyes were bright blue, almost transparent.

"Marios Lakis. I am the liaison for the Ministry of Internal Affairs. I wonder, why are you here, Mr Cole? It was our understanding that you left Cyprus under… shall we say, a cloud, and were not due to return." His accent, like his appearance, was impeccable, having a slight trace of Greek in the inflection of the words, but apart from that his delivery was straight from Kings College. "So, I ask again, why are you here?"

"It's a personal matter."

"There is nothing personal, Mr Cole, especially when it comes to the security of this island. And I do see you as a possible threat to its very balance. Your presence here could unnerve people."

Richard began to think this was about to become akin to the Spanish inquisition any minute now. That Monty Python's Michael Palin would come through the swing doors with a large armchair, shouting, "Nobody expected the Spanish inquisition."

The image brought a sly smile to Richard's face and he looked directly at the man. "I have a friend here, Mr. Lakis. He is going through a very rough divorce and I thought I would come give him moral support."

"Mr Shaw, isn't it? Yes, we have knowledge of this man. He used to fly for the air force I believe, and made some tourist flights, using their property. I also believe, it got him sacked."

The disclosure surprised Richard, he was not aware Peter had been fired for the flight over the rocks, where the story began. "I didn't know."

"Yes, Mr Cole, like so many others here, he too lost his job. A few hundred lost theirs when the incident at the Rocks happened last year. You can't take people to Aphrodite's Rock when there isn't anything to see, can you?"

"I suppose not, and I am sorry. But I didn't know anything about this." Richard's words though genuine fell on deaf ears.

"So, you have come to support your friend, and what else do you plan to do? Resurrect Aphrodite, or perhaps…

Poseidon? Or how about Medusa? All good Greek figures and Gods. Any plans in that direction, Mr Cole?" Lakis' sarcasm bit deep, it was clear Richard's presence was unnerving him.

"Look, Mr Lakis, I am finished with all of that. I just want to go home as soon as I can after I've seen Peter and straighten him out, if I can. He was on the phone to me last week and seemed almost suicidal. I want to help, that's all. Then, as I say, I go home." Richard's voice rose slightly in volume as he pressed his point, his lying convincing. He really had done his best to try justifying his visit. Peter was a good scapegoat for that but more than anything, he had to swerve the idea of any further involvement with Aphrodite's legend. "I am sure if you speak to Lucas Christoulides, he will confirm that I am not a threat."

"You spoke of this man before. Is it not strange that we have no record of him in our administration?"

"And I don't know anything about that, but I met with him. He was at the rocks, he set things up for me."

"No, Mr Cole, the Municipality set things up for you. They were the ones responsible, it came directly from the Mayor's office, and it is the municipality that provided you with the means for you to operate."

"He even sent helpers, came to check on occasion… And what about my work permit, my alien's card?"

"All false. The municipality saw that you were able to generate visitors, so they put the plan into operation overnight. Very innovative of them, wouldn't you say? Who else do you think has the power to do that? It was decided on Saturday and the site closed on the Sunday, yes?"

"Yes, I met Christoulides that day. He told me he did it."

"Whoever you met, Mr Cole, it wasn't him, because he, does not exist." Lakis began to pontificate, his stance one of *'I'm in charge and I say what happens here.'* "No matter, that is in the past, what we have to decide now is if we can allow you to visit us again. I understand your situation and Mr Shaw's, but doubtless, you can appreciate any controversy on your part that could make things bad for you and us. So, we have to think carefully." He mused again as he stretched his finger over his bottom lip. "How long do you think you will need with Mr Shaw?"

"A few days, no more than a week, perhaps ten days. I know he has some things to sort out, property and related subjects." Richard waited for a response.

"We are not unreasonable, and we do empathise with Mr Shaw. These days, a lot of people have taken that final tragic shortcut to debt avoidance, so we will grant you a stay of ten days. I hope that by that time you are back on the plane and off this island. Is this agreeable to you, Mr Cole?"

"Yes, thank you." Richard stood at an angle next to Lakis and offered his hand.

Lakis' hand was clammy, which was an odd surprise to Richard, who had been observing and scrutinising the articulate and well-dressed man with some interest. But the handshake was also proof that this man was either hiding something or not of his word.

Lakis handed Richard his passport, opened the door, and the two walked back out into the corridor.

His case was standing at the end of the hallway, which he collected, walked out past the Customs and 'Nothing to Declare' desks, and into the Arrivals Hall.

A very bored and tired-looking Peter sat on a chair close to the gate.

Richard walked across to him.

Peter stood up and smiled, a warm smile; regardless of why he was there, he was glad to see his old friend.

"I'm sorry, Pete, but they kept me behind, asking questions." Richard took his friend's hand and shook it.

The grip was firm, strong, and solid. Much like Peter himself.

"I thought they might but got here early just in case." And as they walked off, Peter brought the conversation back to normality. "I don't understand why they charge so much for drinks at airports. A bottle of water, almost two Euros, outrageous." He held the bottle in his hand as if it was a precious gold bar. "Come, let's get home, and then you can tell me why you are really here."

Richard climbed into the car, a convertible Renault Meganne. Easing himself into the leather passenger seat, he smiled as he turned to Peter, his look, one of being impressed.

"It's not mine, just borrowing it. My friend, whose place I am looking after, has let me use the car as well. Wants me to make sure it gets a regular run."

Peter's confirmation only merited another smile from Richard, as the car left the airport and sped down the airport road towards Paphos.

"Okay, so now you're back. What is this all about?"

Richard wasn't kidding himself; the questions were going to come quick. "Let's get back to your place. Then we can have coffee and a chat about it. I'd feel better telling you after we both chill a bit."

"Oh, sounds ominous."

Richard kept that thought to himself, his retort of *you don't know how true that is,* ' for his ears only. "What about Sheila?" He turned the question back.

"Yes, let's also leave that till we get back." Peter's reply brought the questioning session to a close, as he turned down the Paphos road and headed back towards town.

Oroklini, evening

Jenny Speagel had called every name in her contact list; no one had seen or heard from Lenny. Her long sleep had also given her a blinding headache, the type she always got when she drank too much red wine. That, and her obvious anxiety at her missing husband had brought some dark thoughts as she scoured through the business cards spread across the table in front of her. He had never been this late before.

She checked the newspaper, there was no football on tonight so he would not be at the pub. There was only one other place she could check. She locked the house, got into her car, and drove about half an hour.

Lenny was known for taking some extra trips, which she didn't want to know about. Sometimes, that cargo was illicit booze, or the odd packet of cannabis, but she never considered him as anything more than an opportunist, never a smuggler, even though she had warned him about it several times. Perhaps this, was one such occasion, where what he had to do was not what he wanted, and something had gone wrong. These thoughts spun through her mind as she drove with her foot firmly down on the accelerator out of Oroklini.

Frimley

Julie waited for the message icon on her phone to light up, and as predicted, it did. Richard's short and succinct two words and one letter message, 'Arrived safe, X' confirmed she could now go up to bed and not worry.

The Meganne cruised easily along the Tomb of the King's Road and turned down past the five-star Elysium Hotel. A few upmarket tourists and what looked like locals were making their way in, dressed in all their finery as they passed by. At the end of the road was a small cul-de-sac, which Peter navigated expertly, squeezing the car through an even narrower gap before parking outside an exclusive villa. The porch lights on the veranda were a cool lemon shade and the patio was spacious with a neatly polished glass-top table and chairs, perfectly set out to catch the bright morning sunshine.

The boot was already open as Peter took out a suitcase and small rucksack and announced. "This is home for the present. Take the end room and leave your gear there. Now, for a couple of beers. I think for starters, Keo?"

"Yes, great." Richard's face confirmed that this was an impressive looking setup and that Peter appeared to have fallen on his feet despite the impending divorce.

"I think you promised you would buy me a crate."

Peter's comment was a sharp reminder of why he was here. So far, the goddess remained quiet, as if biding her time, knowing that up to this moment, he had done all she ordered.

Returning with two large bottles of Keo and two sparkling pint glasses, Peter poured the first beer slowly into Richard's glass.

Richard's eyes followed the smooth movement as the clear amber liquid began to fill the glass, a small head of froth the crowning glory to an expertly poured pint. "Cheers." He drank leisurely as the coldness of the Keo rippled his taste buds and slipped down his throat.

"Okay, I'm waiting." Peter leaned forward on the chair and could not have moved any closer. "Come on, Rich, why are you here?"

All the time Richard was on the plane, he had planned some fabrication on how and what to tell him, but now that he was here, he had no clue where to start. "It's not easy to explain. So, before I do, tell me what happened with you and Sheila?"

"Fine, but don't you believe I am letting you off the hook that easy. Sheila was having an affair." Peter's expression and words seemed almost emotionless, as if he had told the story countless times and become bored with it. And he probably had. "I knew about it, told you as much of my suspicions in the car when you were here, remember? But I thought I'd just let her get it out of her system. We are both at an age where we needed a bit of excitement so I thought the odd fuck might be okay. But then it got serious.

"It really started after you left. Her meetings with this Greek guy became public and she was often spotted out and about arm in arm with him. He wasn't married, had gone through an acrimonious divorce, and had little money left. Sheila didn't know that; thought he was still loaded. He wasn't, his business as a developer had all but collapsed as the housing market over here ground to a halt. After it all came out, we lived apart. But one evening I agreed to meet with her at the local taverna in Pissouri and asked her face to face if she wanted to come back. She said nothing.

"I asked her again, and you know, for one moment, I saw in her eyes just a hint that she was sorry, then it was gone and she left. Or rather, I left. But I couldn't chuck her and the kids out, even though they are away most of the time, so I said she could live at the house and I would find a place. She agreed. Well, she would, wouldn't she?

"Jesus, she hasn't worked in years but that has all changed now and I am not supporting her with the pension I have. She has some cash from her parents' inheritance and it's enough to keep her going till the house gets sold, eventually. It's been on the market for a while so we shall just have to keep our fingers crossed. I moved out and started looking around.

"Then I met up with Tony, an old air force buddy, who opened a broker's place in the City. Did very well and moved into Gold trading, and that's how he's able to fund this lifestyle. He will be back later in the year, but said I could move in and I did, so for now I am house sitting. And that's about it. Sad and a bit shit but there's bugger-all I can do about changing things now, even if I wanted to. Sheila's bed has been well and truly made, laid on, and slept in." Peter sipped from his glass and looked a little melancholic, as if he were recalling his married days. "Okay, well, that's me. Now, tell me why you're here."

"This is not going to be easy to explain. But before I get into it, tell me what happened at the Rocks after we left."

"They simply disappeared. You know that, you were there when it happened."

"Yes, I do. But what happened to the site after that, did people still come?"

"Christ, Rich, the place is more popular than ever, and it's taken on a before and after syndrome. There are even T-shirts with one side Rocks On and the other No Rocks. Why?"

"And Aphrodite's Rock in the water, is it still there?"

"Yes, but protected. They put a steel enclosure under water around that one; no one can get close to it now."

"I wonder why they did that."

"I think they don't want anyone trying to vandalise it or take it away. Remember, the rest of the place is empty now, there are no other rocks there."

Richard picked up his glass and drank it empty.

On cue, Peter opened the second bottle and poured it in.

"What I'm about to tell you is more incredible and crazier than you can imagine, but one other quick question. Are you sure the last night we were here, the night everything changed at the Rocks, you didn't see anything, or anyone?"

"No, only what I heard and saw from a distance. And that was the two of you huddled naked behind the rock on the shore."

"You never saw anything else when you arrived then, anything unusual?"

"Apart from the last rock descending into the water? That was some scary shit." Peter drank slowly while keeping his eyes on Richard. "What do you mean unusual?"

"Something happened that night, something that was the catalyst for all that destruction. The thing is, only Julie and I saw it, which is why it's so difficult to explain."

"Julie saw it too?"

"Yes, so you must believe me when I tell you that what I am about to say is true and real."

Peter reclined in the chair and waited for the revelation, a wry smile creeping from his lips, his mouth poised and open to mock. "Go on, amaze me."

Richard began to narrate the story and there was passion in his words as he tried to convince his friend that the revelation was genuine. "The legend is real, Aphrodite, all of it. She did come out of the water at that spot, created from the foam, born there, as it says in Greek mythology. And how do I know this? Because that night she was in the water with us, Julie and I, and I had to choose between her and my wife. True love, Pete, just like the legend says. I did it and chose Julie."

Peter said nothing.

Richard wondered if it was because he didn't believe him or because he did. He picked up his glass again and sank the rest of the Keo.

"O k a y," Peter's word was spoken slowly as if musing over what he had heard and trying to absorb it.

"I know it's crazy and incredible, but it happened. I swear on my Julie's life it did."

"And she saw it all?" Peter was now going for confirmation.

"Yes, she saw it, and saved me."

"Saved you?"

"Yes, she swam out to the Rock and made me choose."

"You do know how fucking crazy and daft this sounds, don't you? And if it wasn't for the fact that we are mates, I think you could be taking the piss. But let's just say I believe you; it still doesn't explain why you are here now."

"For that, we are going to need something a little stronger."

Zenobia wreck site, 9:30pm

Jenny took the little speedboat out to where they usually anchored off the Zenobia wreck. She had no diving gear on board and toyed with the idea of just taking a free dive, but decided against it. The waves and the sea in general were calm, but there was little moonlight as she skimmed the waves with her torch beam. Nothing. It appeared as if Lenny had not been here after all. Where he was, she could not guess. She stood up in the boat and circled the sea with the torch before switching to the engine and starting the boat again. It was difficult to disguise the fear she felt, but she tried to hide it with some well-timed bravado.

"When he gets back, I'm going to give him hell." She spoke out across the waves. But still nervous of what might be below, she manoeuvred the boat, reversing slightly, and turned it full circle, before heading back to shore. Her composure returning.

As she pulled away, she could just make out the distant sound of a container blasting its warning to approaching ships. The resonance was enough to mask the emergence of a small piece of wood from the depths, the piece that was usually found at the stern of boats, and the name on this one read, 'Jenny's Pride.'

Peter was still listening, saying few words, and watching Richard stand up and move around the patio, his hands and arms moving like windmills as he tried to explain his presence. Mostly, he was impassive, just leaving the room twice; once, to get the brandy bottle that now was under half-full, and the second time, to fetch some nibbles from the kitchen.

Richard's words streamed from him like a confession and he hoped Peter gave him his blessing. As he sat and leaned forward to express himself, Peter poured two more glasses of brandy. The night air seemed too warm around them or it could be the alcohol. Either way, the night and small hours were passing quickly as they sat together.

Peter ran his finger around the tip of the rim; the glass was crystal and sparkled in the light as he lifted it to his lips and sipped, the burn teasing his throat. "Yes, it is as you say, bloody fantastic. So fantastic it's close to impossible to conceive, let alone believe. But let's just say I go along with the idea that the goddess is somehow controlling you. The reports of these two, the boy, and the missing 'Brit', have confirmed that the boy drowned, and the tourist is still missing, also believed drowned. It was in the papers yesterday, and nothing links the two. Besides, how do you think they were killed, if not by drowning? And who's to say the 'Brit' didn't just fuck off with another girl anyway."

"I don't have any evidence other than what she told me, that she did it."

"She told you?" Peter's face was one of incredulity. Could he really give credence to such a wild statement? "Look, Pal, you know I feel a lot for you, and this is not easy for me to say, but I think I should. Your visions and what you hear…" he sipped one more time. "Are you sure it's not a symptom of the PTSD you suffered before? Sure it hasn't just come back? After all, the experience you had on Highway 80 in Kuwait affected you deeply. Christ, it would have affected most people. Not many would have come through that unscathed. We all read about it in the papers and saw the images on the news, but you were there, saw it all happen. I can only guess what you went through. Remember what the Doctor told us? You were suffering from a form of schizophrenia."

"Yes, I know, but I never told you the entire story. Maybe if I did, it would have been easier for me to cope, with someone else knowing what I saw."

"What about your sergeant? He was there."

"He was. But once the shelling started, he went back to the jeep to report. I was the only one left to observe, and it happened all at once after that."

"What did you see, Richard?" Peter sat back in the chair to listen.

Richard's eyes glazed, as if swollen with tears. The tears of memories he wanted to forget, never really could, and came rushing back. How many times had he relived it? It was like a one-act play that repeated itself over and over and it always started the same way. As he began to retell it, the images played out before him. Even as he spoke, the pictures were as clear as the day he first saw them. The jeep ride across the desert and the approach towards Highway 80. He turned back to Peter as if he had suddenly hit the pause button on the recorder.

"A woman killed herself in front of me. Blew herself up just to kill an American soldier. I think she blew her baby up too… it happened so quick…" He stuttered over the pictures in his mind. "I never thought I would see…" He picked up his glass, now refilled, and swallowed slowly. "You know, I actually thought…" His speech was nervy, he began to miss words, and his senses began to give way to the images. "I thought I would get through it… without a scratch. Fuck! How naïve was I? I know I have no divine right to say that, and why should I? I knew it was part of my job, dying! But that day, it wasn't a job, or a vocation, it wasn't even part of being a soldier. This was slaughter and cold-blooded murder, disguised as war; dirty, disgusting, and delusional. And as I sat there watching, I wondered what it must be like to be in that column of 2,000 vehicles and thousands of people. Trapped, unable to move, unable to go back, or forward; men, women, and children, all locked together in one long line of despair and terror. With nowhere to run, or hide, stuck on one long straight road to oblivion, practice targets for an unseen enemy. Picked off without any thought for whom or what they were killing."

"They chose to fight, mate. They could have surrendered." Peter's retort was a defensive one.

"You think they chose? Really? They were running. And surrender was not an option either, they had no choice at all. Okay, maybe there were Republican Guards in the convoy, or maybe they were just conscripts, given guns and forced to shoot at us…"

"It was war, Richard. Things like this happen in war."

"War, you say. So, what is our protocol? We shoot back, kill, or be killed, you say, and for what, God, Queen, and

Country? Most of those who were in that column, were trying to escape. I saw dead mothers, holding onto their dead sons. Soldiers in their trucks burnt alive, their heads etched into the metal of vehicles, moulded together in steel and flesh, twisted wrecks of humanity, unrecognisable as a name, or a person…" Richard drew a deep breath, remembering the horrific sights. "After the shells stopped and it was all over, I got up from the sanctuary I was holed up in and walked among them. I can still see it now, feel it too. I can even remember the acrid smell of the smoke; it still fills my nostrils. The bitter churning smoke that strangled my breathing and coated my eyes in drops of water.

"As I pushed through the smoke and emerged into the carnage, I had the weirdest feeling. It felt like I was in an art gallery, with all the pieces around me, all part of a great exhibition, with each individual life and death captured in that moment. And among all that wanton desolation there was one abiding image that stayed with me, still haunts me even today. Out of all the horrors I saw that day, an Iraqi woman lay dead next to a young soldier, her arms clutched around his neck as if she were embracing him, cradling him to her. I believe she was his Mother, the one who brought him into the world, and was now with him as he left it. And she wouldn't let him die alone, because in that scene, the two most significant events in that boy's life were captured and framed for all to see; the one who gave him life and the place where it was taken away. His Mother was there with him throughout and she wasn't about to let go."

Peter sank the last remnants of his brandy and placed a hand on Richard's shoulder. "I'm glad you told me. And perhaps it's about time you put this story and yourself to bed. It's been a long day and tomorrow we will have a think about what we can do next."

"That's not the end of the story. There's something else I never told you, or anyone else, not even Julie."

Peter sat back down on the sofa and poured the leftover Remy into the crystal glass.

"This may be for you the hardest to believe, I don't believe it either, but it happened."

"Get on with it then. I need my beauty sleep."

"After the woman dressed in black blew the kid up, another woman appeared, and much more sinister looking. She too was clothed in black, but her garments were long flowing and dragged along the ground. She stared at me and began to walk towards me. I got up, and started running away, as fast as I could. But when I turned around, she was practically next to me. Then, a mist formed ahead of me and I ran straight into it, thinking it was the smoke from the massacre. But as it cleared, I found myself on the beach at Petra Tou Romiou, and before me was yet another woman. I knew who it was, without even thinking about it. Aphrodite. She stood there naked and spoke to me."

"What did she say?" Peter was gripped by the unfolding tale.

"I will always keep you safe. I tried to call to her but the next thing I knew I was back in my bunk bed. Then, you came in."

"It was a dream, a follow on from your Highway experience. That's all."

"No, it was more than that. And that's why when I saw her on the beach, I recognised her instantly, and why she said, *you know who I am, Richard."*

"Well, I admit, it is spooky, but I still think it's a symptom of your PTSD. You really do need to see someone about that. Look how many years it's been, and it still haunts you."

"You're right, and I will see someone as soon as we get this sorted. Thanks, Pete." Richard stood and shook his friend's hand; glad he had made his confession. "You are right about bed too; I am knackered now."

The two men left the patio and made their way to their respective bedrooms; both were en-suite so there was no waiting around to use the facilities.

Richard stripped quickly and turned the shower on. The temperature rose as the hot streams filled the tiled shower floor and the vapour piped rapidly to the ventilator. He climbed in, moved under the fresh jets of steaming water, and let them cascade down his body as he smothered himself in a cool blue shower gel. He closed his eyes, recalling his conversation with Peter, and how he had been candid and honest. But in that steam, he also recalled those images of how he had walked through the smoke, the aftermath of the attack, and how the solitary figure of the woman dressed in black pursued him until his goddess stepped forward to save him.

"I will keep you safe, Richard, always."

He was sure that was not the case now. She wanted him, true, but more than that, she wanted revenge.

CHAPTER NINE

Getting out of hand

Cyprus beaches vary, some are shingle, some are sandy, and others are a mix of sand and shingle. But the beaches of Protaras and Ayia Napa are golden, with sand so fine and glorious in colour and texture that they could have been ripped from the pages of tropical travel brochures.

The only other element that compliments these glorious beaches is the sea itself. This part of the Mediterranean is majestic, with colours that diverge with time and tide and always unpredictably. One day, its hues are green like emeralds, the next it becomes a glistening shimmer of sapphires, encrusted with ermine that hems the top of the waves.

From dawn, slices of amber bristle against the dark blues of a dying night to herald the arrival of a new day. By dusk, as the sun begins to set, colder greys form against the pink of the diminishing horizon as darkness looms, to draw its blanket of night over the sun-drenched ocean. This transfusion of colour makes this coast special and confirms why so many people choose to holiday here each year, relaxing and lazing on its fourteen blue-flagged beaches.

This recognition of excellence also offers another title for the tourist office, that of 'young person's haven and playground for the youth.' Given, it has some of the trendiest and in-demand clubs and bars on the island. And whilst it is true that Ayia Napa caters to these upwardly mobile, iPhone carrying clientele, Ayia Napa is not exclusively theirs. Families love the place too, especially the beaches, one of the favourites being the famous Nisi Beach.

One such family who chose Nisi to spend their days, were the Kellys; Steven and Haley, with their two kids, Josh, and Katy. Katy was the youngest at just three, and Josh older by three years, at six. Both loved the sea and both adored the sand. They were good kids, who did not quarrel often, but when they did it was usually about little things, like who had the bigger lolly or 'that's what I wanted', which was nearly always the opposite of the other one. But generally, they were well-behaved, unlike some of the little monsters in their apartment complex.

Ayia Napa, Thursday morning

Steven got up early and found a good site close to the beach bar and the water. He had left the apartment to go down straight after breakfast to find the perfect spot and get a couple of beach loungers.

Haley brought the kids about twenty minutes later and as they started to unwrap and unravel their various beach toys, towels, buckets and spades, the beach around them began to fill up. She leaned into her large plastic bag and brought forth a collection of tubes, bottles, and more tubes. This was her sun safety kit, each one with a factor of protection higher than the next, most in their thirties, others, forties, even fifties, and when applied, offered a smattering of protective goo that was rapidly spread across the kids' bodies, embalming them from head to foot. She believed one couldn't be too careful with sunscreens.

Steven on the other hand, just took a splodge of cream and spread it without hesitation across his legs, body, and face, yellow streaks still visible as he waited for Haley to rub it into his back, shoulders, and thighs.

Haley, now satisfied with her family's protection, applied the cream much more delicately to her own body and face as if she were applying makeup.

Josh was the first to head for the water, carrying with him a small plastic inflatable in the shape of a turtle. Katy's was more ladylike and in the shape of a dolphin. Josh entered the sea and let the water creep up his body as he made his way further into the waves. Stephen held Haley's hand as she gingerly stepped in then offered it to Katy as she held onto her mother's other hand and the two of them swung her back and forth into the waves, her giggling ringing out across the beach.

Their belongings safely tucked away under the beach chairs, the Kellys were now thoroughly enjoying the day. Security on these beaches is almost surreptitious, like an unwritten rule that those who are in the water have someone on shore looking after their stuff; it's the etiquette of the beach, the odd thing is, it seems to work.

But with a mere glance towards his son, Steven became anxious as the young boy began to move farther away from him.

Josh had let his turtle go and it had now begun drifting away from the shore, so he kept moving forward, his feet barely treading water.

His father shouted after him. "Josh, not too far."

Josh seemed oblivious to his Father's shout, as the beach-shelf started to undulate and the water began creeping up his young body. He was barely above the surface, as the water cloaked him in.

Steven moved away from Haley and Katy and began to swim towards his son, who, for some reason, now stood perfectly still. He swam faster and then faster still with a somewhat awkward freestyle stroke, but it served its purpose as it took him closer to Josh quickly.

Still, the boy had not moved.

His Father, sensing how close he was, grabbed at him. "Don't you ever…" but before he could say another word, Josh turned, holding something in his hand, which Steven instantly recognised, and it chilled him as he snatched it out of the small hand. Not sure what to do with it, he let it fall into the water, took hold of Josh, and carried him back, holding him tight.

In the distance, the inflatable turtle floated out to sea.

As if synchronized, the unexpected piece of flotsam floated alongside them towards the shore, now revealed as the severed arm and hand of a man.

Haley watched nervously, unsure of what was happening, as Steven moved quickly through the water with Josh in his arms, hugging and squeezing him tight against his chest.

People around them began to stop, to stand, and stare at the water, as obvious signs of distress emanated from both Father and son. The boy clinging to the man, his tears and sobs unnerving and audible.

"Haley, what's the number for the police? We've got to call them."

There was then a scream, which echoed down and around the beach, and the chance discovery was now public knowledge.

At last, something of Barry Rochester had been found.

Protaras

The Marinara Apartments, Protaras, were empty and quiet, as Greg, Chrissy, and Mary carried their suitcases down the stairs; their taxi to the airport was booked for 10:30am.

Greg placed the four suitcases in a line. Barry's, he moved to one side.

Kristina, the Manageress, came from behind the reception desk. A petite woman, she was dressed in a smart red and black dress, with a pair of shiny black shoes, and coiffed hair, which made her look older than she was. Her expression was mellow, as she was only too aware of the situation. She smiled, somewhat nervously at Greg, uncertain what to say.

He didn't acknowledge her right away, instead, he grabbed the handle of Barry's suitcase, and lifted it up, unsure what to do with it.

Kristina took it from his hand. "We shall put it away for when he returns. Don't worry, it will be safe with us." Her English was very good, but it was still tinged with a Cypriot accent.

Greg nodded and said nothing, his expression enough to confirm his gratitude.

Chrissy checked her watch, 10:35am. The sound of the taxi horn outside meant the holiday was officially over, although, for her and the others, it had ended the day they went to Cape Greco.

Paphos
Peter had prepared a late breakfast, consisting of Halloumi and Lounza, with a couple of boiled eggs, some fresh Greek bread, duly toasted, tea and orange juice, and a small plate of black olives.

Both sat in the same chairs as the night before and neither said much as they ate their fare, just trading the odd sentence or two, but making no in-depth exchange. Possibly, both were waiting for the right moment to speak their mind.

Last night's conversation had been a heavy one and had opened a chasm between them, one that was growing bigger with every passing second and in order to break that impasse, one of them had to say something.

Peter picked up his cup of tea, sipped it, then dipped the last corner of his toast into the cup before eating it.

"You have a great place here, now that I've seen it in the daylight." The silence was broken. "Some location too, only a stone's throw from the beach." Richard finished his tea, sat back, took his phone out, and said, "I think I should call Julie."

Peter placed the cup on the table and fixed his eyes on his friend, knowing he had to ask the million-dollar question. "What exactly are you going to do?" His question was more like a statement. "If what you told me last night has any truth to it, and you do know how incredible that sounds, don't you?" He paused, reflecting on the words he had just uttered, then repeated. "If it does, what are you going to do?"

Richard's mobile phone began to ring, the tone seeming almost insistent. He picked it up, the screen read, private number. He answered and waited for the voice on the other end to speak.

"Mr Cole, I see you are back in Cyprus."

Richard looked straight at Peter and mouthed. "It's Christoulides. Hello, yes… I was trying to contact you." He paused, thinking about his next sentence. "But when I got here the authorities told me you don't exist."

"How is that, Mr Cole? I am talking to you now."

"Yes, well, I mean… they said you didn't exist or were where I said you were." Richard's nerves began to jangle; Christoulides had a way of making him feel uneasy.

"Mr Cole, my office is not in the directory, I work in different areas, and guises. This allows me certain advantages and freedoms."

"I see." Richard didn't seem convinced.

"I want to meet tonight, Mr Cole, 7:30pm, at the House of Dionysus. You can find it easily. And do come alone."

"Yes, sure, 7:30pm." Richard felt the same authority from Christoulides as he did the first time they met. As he put the phone down, his mind wandered back to that meeting. "He said he will meet me tonight at half past seven, and to come alone."

"Fuck me, Richard, you do love a drama." Peter's somewhat awkward smile and the call cleared the fog between them and now one of them had a purpose, which would undoubtedly also involve the other.

"I am to meet him at the House of Dionysus. Do you know it?"

Peter nodded. "That's neat, it's a fantastic ancient villa with amazing mosaics, both Greek and Roman covering the floors, depicting scenes from mythology. It's a great place dedicated to the god of wine, so this will be right up your street. And it's not far, just by the harbour. It won't take more than ten minutes to get there."

"You can run me there then."

"Of course. Don't I always?"

"I'll call Julie now. I think our court case will be adjourned for another week, if that is okay with you. It could just get a little interesting from now on."

Peter smiled and poured another cup of tea for them both.

Nicosia, same day

The Nicosia sun is hotter than in most cities in Cyprus, and the temperature often touches several degrees higher than the rest of the country, but after dusk, the evenings are cool, and humidity lower than in other places. It compensates for the day and it makes Nicosia a pleasant place to live, work, and a great place to rest, relax or dine out, and be entertained just like any other modern cosmopolitan capital city.

It is also the hub of the country with most of the government positioned there, as well as the municipal and state offices. It is where Panayotis Linos and Christina Skalos have their offices, whilst Francoise Mulot and Gregor Tabachi are both based in Limassol, and although separated by distance, all had just learnt of the discovery of the severed arm at Ayia Napa and each was acting upon the news in their own way.

"Yes, that's right; I want you to find the Minister now." Linos' raised voice couldn't disguise the depth of worry that his furrowed brow reflected. "Alright, if that's the case I will come and see him personally… Yes, I know what time it is and I don't care if IT IS LUNCH TIME." He slammed the telephone down just as his mobile began to ring, his *Zorba the Greek* tune totally out of synch with the situation.

"Hello, Christina. Yes, I just heard they closed the beach at Nisi… about half an hour ago; the police are all over the place, along with forensics… Yes, it's sealed off so the people were told to leave and find another place. What do they think this is, Amity? Oh, the kid? He's okay, just upset and his Father says he will be fine. I hope so too. Christina… has anyone else spoken to you? Oh… what did she say? Well, yes… we did say if anything else was to happen… but this is quite unexpected… Yes, they are sure it's the British tourist… the police have a picture of him and he had a watch tattoo on his wrist… Yes, a watch tattoo… like a watch… that's right… Well, I'm going to see the Minister now… do you want to come along? Right, perhaps you'd better speak to Gregor as well, but I expect he has already been told. And if I hear anything, I will call you, and you do the same. I just hope the media don't make a huge thing of this… yes, alright… bye."

CHAPTER TEN

Between a rock and a hard place

Richard checked his watch as he sat in the car waiting for Peter. It was almost seven pm, plenty of time to get there.

It was odd, but he had a deep appreciation for Christoulides, which bordered on respect in a sort of officer-type role, just like during his time in the Army, something he hadn't been involved with for a few years. Perhaps he should salute Christoulides the next time he met him. That thought was quickly dismissed as the local Cyprus station Rock-FM started banging out its latest hit, after which the news would follow.

Peter climbed in and turned the volume dial up just as the news intro began.

"The authorities in Ayia Napa are treating the recent discovery of the dismembered arm as nothing more than a tragic boating accident. No official announcement has been made as to the identity of the body part, but it is thought to be that of the missing British tourist, Barry Rochester, who has been missing for about seven days, and is believed to have drowned. This is the second person, in the past few weeks, to have gone missing in these coastal waters. Just recently, a nine-year old Romanian boy was also found in a similar state, again alleged to be an accident, although Police have not completely ruled out foul play. A spokesman for the Municipality has assured people that the waters off Ayia Napa are totally and utterly safe and accidents like this are rare, but there is always a chance of something occurring, especially if a person gets into difficulty and becomes trapped in the sea lanes. In other news… Progress continues with the Open Factory idea for the continued bid for Paphos Cultural City 2017, but the recent bailout crisis has put a great strain on resources, a spokesman for the project said today."

Peter leaned in to turn off the radio. "Paphos won that bid to host the Cultural City, against Limassol and Nicosia. All very proud, we were. Although they haven't done much with the rock, no need to I suppose, they get enough people going there every day now, more than when the rocks were there. All your fault." Peter laughed as Richard looked at him a little sheepishly. "I'm going to park and then go get a drink. You can walk from here, it's about five hundred metres just off the harbour. I will meet you back here at *The Cafe on the Corner*."

"Where?"

"The Cafe on the Corner, that's what it's called, bloody tourist." He smirked at Richard's ignorance of the town.

"Oh, okay, right. I will see you back there then."

Peter shut the car door and Richard left, moving down the hill and on to the seafront. He passed several tourists and locals, who seemed to stare at him, before turning away; a reaction he was getting used to.

The sun was setting low in the sky as he approached the gate, only to find it locked and a notice in English, Greek, Russian, and Chinese that read 'closed'. He looked around the outside of the villa, it was deserted. But just as he was about to turn and walk back to the harbour, he heard the unmistakable voice of Christoulides.

"Leaving so soon, Mr Cole?"

"Oh, hi, I saw the door was shut, so I thought…"

"That I wasn't coming."

"Yes."

"Don't you know by now that when I say something I mean it? I arranged to have a private visit of the villa, away from prying eyes, as I suspect you have noticed that your presence has raised a few eyebrows already. There is much to show you and discuss but before we start this tour, I need you to tell me exactly what happened at the rocks the last time you were here. And I do mean from the beginning, from the moment you first saw the figure in the sea."

As he listened, Richard noticed how much Christoulides' English had improved and how eloquent his words were. "From the beginning? Surely you know the story by now, the papers were full of it." His comment outlined how unnecessary he thought this was.

"Yes, Mr Cole, but I want to hear it from your own lips, not from a third-party media."

Both men sat on a wooden bench just in front of the entrance. Richard began to speak, while his companion sat back and closed his eyes, as if he were translating the words into pictures in his head. Christoulides didn't say anything, merely listened.

He tried to keep his tone normal, but it was difficult to keep his emotions in check as he recalled the past and the very reason why he was back again. As he completed his story, Christoulides rose from the bench and looked down at him.

Richard noticed how much the man's appearance and demeanour had changed outwardly since their last meeting. True, his understanding and English speech had somehow become excellent, but there was also something else different about him, because whilst he still maintained that same patriarchal look, as if he were the 'Daddy' of all he surveyed, his face looked older, and his eyes tired. Whatever responsibilities he carried on his shoulders, were beginning to take their toll on him.

"It is without doubt a fascinating tale, and the fact that your wife also witnessed the same makes it more plausible. And however difficult it is for others to believe, I believe you. Now, alas, it would seem your story continues, Mr Cole."

Richard's surprise was clear, he positively did not expect this from Lukas. And his endorsement of what had transpired was even more unexpected, because all he was prepared for was a comment along the lines of, "come off it, Mr Cole", or whatever the equivalent was in Greek. Presently, four people knew what had taken place and up until today, only one appeared to still be sceptical. That Christoulides seemed convinced of its authenticity, was something of a relief.

"Perhaps you are asking yourself why I believe you."

"Yes. Actually… yes, I was, especially as I have no proof."

"Your proof is the disappearance of the rocks. Do you think something like that can be attributed to nature, even though that is the common belief of the masses? No, Mr Cole, that alone sets you aside from the idea that what happened was a natural disaster. Which is why, I suspect you are the magnet for all the tragedy the island is currently experiencing. Come with me, let me show you something."

Richard walked one pace behind Christoulides, before he saddled up to stand beside him as Lukas played tourist guide to his single audience member.

Christoulides pushed the gate open and they walked in. "This villa is dedicated to Dionysus, the god of wine. You may not know it, but Cyprus was one of the very first countries to cultivate wines, as long ago as five thousand years. The grapes grow well in the soil here and there are many vineyards that produce even today some of the finest vintages."

Richard listened carefully as Lukas began enjoying his new role.

"No one knows who this villa belonged to; perhaps some rich Roman, or a well-to-do citizen of the town. Either way, the mosaics are magnificent, and remind me of a time long past."

Richard watched him as he spoke; there was a certain gentleness to his speech, which was out of character with his usual bravado.

"Follow me, Mr Cole, it is just through here."

Richard stepped inside.

The sun, at its nadir, gave way to a blossoming moonlight, casting a glittering radiance into the room, bathing the floor in a mix of natural and artificial light that highlighted the ornate features of the classical scenes. The pillars surrounding the mosaics became like stone sentries, solid, and impressive.

"Come closer, Mr Cole. This is the oldest mosaic here, older by some five hundred years, it is important that you study it closely."

Richard drew near to the stone picture. It was grainier than the rest and did indeed look older. Around its edges, small cracks had formed, emphasising its age, and at the centre of the design was a faded image, one that he could not distinguish clearly.

"What you told me of Aphrodite and her emergence from the sea has much to do with this representation before you. When the goddess stepped on the shore to be with you, she left her sanctuary, becoming almost mortal. This, of course, is only my interpretation, you understand? Your rejection of her, made her realise she did not have as much control as she thought she had over you and that of her dominion. Only by reasserting her power would she be able to recapture that, and you.

"But she also knew you would not come to her willingly, that you had to be persuaded or cajoled in whatever way she could find to make sure you returned. It is my belief the goddess has misused her authority to conjure up one of the deadliest creatures from the depths to become her tool for this purpose. The Scylla. And that is what you see before you. Because, Mr Cole, Aphrodite has once again left her sanctuary to walk among the mortals. Only this time, she has vengeance in her heart, not love. She seeks to torture you, to make you submit to her, to make you her slave, to destroy you and your world, and unless you do something about it, that will be your destiny."

Richard felt a shiver run down his back, as if the fingernail of truth had drawn a line across his soul. Taking all of Lukas' words in, he realised that possibly, he still had more to tell. He sat down on the cold floor, looked up at Lukas, and asked only one question. "How do you know all this?"

"I know this because I believe it is the truth. And perhaps you too recognise the situation more than you care to. Did you not sense that when she spoke to you? She has the ability to make men do as she wants, always has. Her seductive powers grip all the senses and twist them, so that even if you try to resist as you have, she simply grips tighter. She has proven that already because, here you are, is that not so?"

"Yes, I suppose so."

Lukas had skilfully avoided the question.

Richard asked again. "But how do you know this?"

"For now, this is all you need to know, when the time comes, I will tell you how. But first, you must face your own questions, the ones you need answers for. Once you have those, you will be ready to learn the truth. You are, Mr Cole, stuck between a rock and a hard place, and soon you will discover the significance of that phrase. Study the image and the Scylla, for one day soon you may have to face it, along with your other demons."

Richard moved closer to the rendition on the floor; even the faded image carried an ominous presence. Taking his cell phone from his pocket, he scrolled down the menu until he found camera, zoomed in, and began to click and shoot from different angles. As he finished the last shot, he turned around and found the room empty. Lukas had, in his customary way, vanished without a word. Getting to his feet, Richard moved out of the room, through the entrance, and out of the gate, closing it behind him.

As he walked towards *The Cafe on the Corner,* he mused over Christoulides' words and how he had offered his own theory, which, had created more questions, ones he had no answers for, but somehow needed to find.

Peter sat in a corner, towards the back of the café, and had a large Keo bottle in front of him, which was always good value and better for sharing. He poured the beer into Richard's glass. "You found him okay then?" He asked and shuffled his chair to allow Richard more room at the table.

The hubbub from the café grew a little quieter as Richard sat down, as if people in the establishment were keen on eaves-dropping on their chat. "Yes, I saw him, and he had a lot to say. But we can talk about it later, back at your place."

"Sure. Well, let's finish these and then we will make a move, unless you want to eat here?"

"No, better at home, and a sandwich is fine." Richard chinked his cold beer glass against Peter's. "Cheers."

Both drank slowly.

Christoulides left the villa without another word to Richard, for emphasis on the dramatic was his calling card. Moving down the harbour and away from the crowded pavements, he climbed the small hill-road, which carried little traffic this time of night. Walking unhurriedly in the opposite direction of the town, he paused as a familiar sound interrupted his thoughts.

"Do you really think you can stop me?" Aphrodite's voice carried across the wind to where Lukas stood at the side of the road.

"I will try. But for now, it is enough that I am able to keep you from him."

"For how long? Your power grows weaker, and you are not what you were. I sense it and I know you do too." The mocking tone cut deep.

"What you have done is against the code of the Gods. You have used your power to satisfy your own lust and selfishness. You have taken a creature from the depths to act as your aide in your schemes and created a bridge between mortals and immortals, breaking all the rules."

"That may be so, but I will still have him."

"Not if he says no. You cannot make him, no matter what you do. It is his conscience and soul that makes that decision, not your connivance. You know as well as I that only a willing soul will capitulate. It cannot be forced."

"We shall see, Father."

Peter sat on the sofa, Richard stood at the front of the patio, and a discarded pizza box littered the small glass coffee table.

"That's me stuffed..." Peter wiped away the last remnants of tomato sauce from his mouth with a white serviette and opened his laptop. "You wanted to show me something?"

"I need to download these pictures from the camera. I've got a lead."

Peter leaned down, took the lead, and placed it in the socket of the laptop and into the camera.

Richard began to download the images and created a new file. "I hope they came out alright." He waited for the last to copy over then clicked on the first one.

"Haven't we done this before?" Peter's rhetorical comment struck a chord with both.

Richard opened the first image and enlarged it by 150 percent. "What the..."

The word fuck wasn't needed, the open-mouthed expression on both of their faces confirmed its presence anyway. And the other images only added more mystique and mystery to the images unfolding before them.

Richard returned to the first one, as that particular one seemed the sharpest of all. He again enhanced it up to a level where the image remained sharp and in focus. "Lukas calls it a Scylla; it's a mythical creature of Ancient Greek mythology."

"Christ, it's ugly, hideous…" Peter's words were correct as he ran his finger over the outline of the creature, careful to avoid touching the screen.

The figure consisted of a woman's head and face with a body made up of dogs or wolves' heads protruding like some alien being from her stomach. Several of her legs were shaped like tentacles and wrapped around her lower body whilst others stretched out, ready to grab any prey and drag it closer to the dogs' fangs, huddled in her abdomen. As if that wasn't enough, the creator of this vile being had given her arms that resembled the claws of a giant crab, with deadly suckers underneath, that gripped and sucked on the bare flesh of its victims.

"She is one ugly mother." Peter's comment summed up the image perfectly.

"Lukas says I will need to face her if I am to survive." Richard glanced at Peter, knowing he had said too much and wished he had bitten his tongue, but it was too late already.

"Oh, wait a minute now. You're not telling me that you believe this thing is alive? Do you?" Peter's incredulity bordered on hilarity as his face moved from wry smile to total laughter. He could not contain himself.

It was infectious and Richard too began to smirk, then smile, and then laugh, as he also saw the funny side of the situation.

"I have seen and heard some things since we first met, but this… this is the best. Just like one of those Ray Harry thing-me-bob films from the 60's. And I suppose you are Jason and I'm one of the Argonauts. Fuck me, Richard, you are priceless, so priceless." Peter began to laugh harder.

Their chortling broke into short giggles as the two grew louder, the volume and fits of hilarity evidence of the funny side.

"Oh, yeah, and you know what?" Richard's body began to rock and roll on the sofa.

Peter slapped Richard hard on the back and gripped him around one shoulder, their voices raucous and uncontrolled. Small tears began to roll from his eyes. "You were saying…" He tried to keep some element of calm as he spoke.

"Pete, my mate, you are going to help me find it. Ah ha, what do you think about that?" Richard rolled against the sofa as his last comment brought forth the biggest roar from them both.

CHAPTER ELEVEN

A storm is coming

Nicosia, Friday, 8am

The clouds turned from white to black within a few seconds, as they passed over the tops of houses and offices in Nicosia. The day's morning sunshine temporarily ended as a storm began to brew around the city. But this was not the only storm that was taking place that morning. The raised voices and heated exchanges emanating from the conference room of the Minister of the Interior's office, were nearly as loud as the periodic claps of thunder that interrupted the vitriolic words that echoed across the Minister's desk, most of them coming from Panayotis Linos, as he held court whilst the rest of the room, a mix of interested parties, remained silent.

"Do you realise this decision will not only affect the resort but could also threaten the investment programme for the Marina and other developments? It's financial suicide. So, what if one stupid British Tourist drowns? It happens all the time. Sad, but it happens, and we cannot jeopardise our plans for the region. The press and media are just waiting for another disaster and I don't have to tell you what their reaction will be. Look what happened last time, and we are still paying for it. Another wrong decision like that and we will all be joining the unemployment line. Isn't it bad enough that we must live with this austerity chain around our necks? It's hard just trying to keep our heads above water, but this is dragging us deeper into the flood of despair. Anymore, and we will drown for sure." Panayotis sat down, his speech delivered, and he, out of breath.

Heracles Aristides was the man most of the comments were aimed at.

As Minister for the Interior and Tourism, he carried a lot of responsibilities that reflected the burden of his office, and he did it with a certain panache, which his fifty-plus years on the planet had given him. He had a gift for listening, assessing, and evaluating, before finally commenting.

He was as smart in dress as he was astute. Except now, he was beginning to show his age; his hair-line having begun receding quite rapidly over the past few months, which made him look older. His crow's feet were visibly defined around his eyes and his skin, ruddy, as if he was permanently in a state of embarrassment. Not tall or short, but somewhere in the middle, his stature was decidedly middle of the road. For all the right reasons, Heracles Aristides made a good civil servant.

He stood up, moved from behind his desk, and walked across to the window, practically ignoring the people in the room as he stood looking out. The bulk of the clouds above the skylight stayed dark and ominous, but just to the left, a small ray of sunlight began to peak from under the bottom of the nearest cloud.

"Panayotis…" Heracles turned to address him. "You use a good metaphor for the position we are in, drowning. I too share your concern and appreciate your passion in registering your disapproval of my decision, but there is more at stake than the immediate problems. God knows we've had to battle in recent times with elements that are not all of our making, and continue to do so, but this is one battle we cannot shy away from. This is the time where we must show our face, not hide from the press and media. The time where we must load the ammunition we wish to fire, not what is best for the weapon. You see, I too can use metaphors." He moved from the window to face Panayotis. "Allow me to explain. If we were to simply march on without recourse to this tragic incident, and allow the beaches to reopen immediately, we would be acknowledging this event as something that, as you say, happens. Of course, the police and their forensic teams must do their investigations, but I understand that this is almost complete; so, we could just reopen the beaches, yes?"

Panayotis nodded his approval and interjected Heracles flow. "That's what I want."

"I know, but that is not what we will do. We must consider the bigger picture and I don't mean your investors, I mean the country's reputation. We have close to three million guests each year, give, or take, for the past ten years, visiting this island. We expect to have more, much more, once the Oil and Gas begins to flow and the economy booms again. Do you think that we should simply say, as you put it, though not so candidly, one stupid British tourist drowns, but we still carry on? What does that demonstrate to the world? It shows no respect, that all we care about is money. Yes, there will be some short-term losses, but the media will focus on the benevolence of the government and the local authorities to esteem and value human life. It is, after all, just short term.

"I have arranged for a brief memorial service this Sunday for the man, and the young Romanian boy, who also drowned a while ago, to show that we are not only aware of the situation but we also share their loss. This will give people an opportunity to reflect and for you to make sure that your investors are fully briefed on the actions that this department has taken. By early next week, we shall reopen the beaches. As I say, it is unavoidable but necessary. And I expect you to carry out this… shall we say, request, Panayotis." Heracles returned to the window as the sunshine pierced the clouds, introducing the rooftops of Nicosia to a bright blue sky morning. "I believe the storm has passed." Then he moved back to sit behind his desk.

Panayotis felt as if he had been battered into submission by a pair of invisible boxing gloves, and although he couldn't see the bruises he certainly felt them. He left the Minister's office with his ego deflated and his pride dented.

Richard and Peter spent the morning tidying up; it was surprising how with only the two of them in the house it had become decidedly scruffy. But all the time they were busy domesticating themselves with scrubbing-brush, Hoover, and dustpan, their conversation stayed distinctly on the one topic. Who or what were they looking for.

Peter sat on the lounge chair and poured himself another large cup of black filtered coffee. It had the desired effect, as he felt his head take on a different type of banging, instead of the hangover variety; this one seemed not as noisy and offered just a hint of normality returning.

"Well, that's me done." Richard too sat down and reached for the pot, adding milk and one spoonful of sugar to his brew, then stirred slowly, making sure the spoon didn't clash with the cup.

Peter finished his coffee and leaned back. He had printed the images and two of them were laid out on the table in front of them. "If nothing else, I think I should try find out a bit more about this Scylla creature. I will spin into town and go to the villa. Maybe I can talk to someone there and get some more information. You never know."

"Good idea. You might even see Christoulides."

"I never have, so far."

"What?" Richard queried the statement.

"Seen Christoulides… I have never seen him, or met him."

"Is that so? I felt sure you had."

"Nope, you seem to be the only one who has."

Richard mused for a second, reconfirming Peter's last answer. He was right, thus far, he was the only one who had spoken to Christoulides. Next time they met, he would be sure to take Peter along; although, he wasn't sure when that would be, as Christoulides had left no message about when or where to contact him.

Peter grabbed the keys, collected his short denim bomber-jacket, and made his way to the front door. "I suggest you have a dig around too, see what you can find out about what we are dealing with here, might help eventually. Have a look on the web as well, I'll bet you'll find quite a bit there. Okay, help yourself to whatever. See you later, I won't be long."

"Bye." Richard's word was lost as the door closed.

Pulling the laptop over to him, he clicked on Google, and typed in Scylla. As soon as he hit the keys, a vast array of websites filled the screen. *This may take a while,* he thought.

The Nicosia Morgue had been quite busy over the past week. With Nicos' accident and the recent discovery of the now confirmed, by forensics, Barry Rochester's body part, Elena had her hands full in more ways than one. Plus, she was on her own most of the time, as her other two colleagues were absent—one was away on a seminar in Bosnia whilst the other was off sick—leaving her to pick up all the bits and pieces and all the other human offal that fermented on her steel 'table of death', as it was affectionately known.

She also had not given herself much time to grieve, but when it was quiet, the tears often flowed at the thought of Nicos; taken so young, and so tragically.

Her schedule allowed her little time for an in-depth review of Mr. Rochester's arm and fingers, so she simply checked all the visible signs and filed him away into the cold cabinet. Whether it was time constraints, she felt tired, or she just wasn't concentrating, there was something odd about Rochester's dismembered limb. Something that a trained Detective would have spotted, but she missed as the cabinet slid into its metal recess. On closer inspection, she might have noticed that Barry's hand was closed tight, as if it had gripped something. But Elena packed him away without opening it, as the fist seemed impossible to pry open. Had she done so, she would have discovered one piece of evidence; a small scale, that once inside that cold dark cabinet, began to glow.

London, Angel Islington, same day

Chrissy received the call just about an hour after they reached the flat in Islington. Greg and Mary had gone back with her, and as they had all been together during the past week, in many ways, it seemed kind of natural that they would be together when the phone call came through. It wasn't as if she wasn't expecting it but when it became official, it was still a shock.

She had spoken for just a couple of minutes, her main question to the police, if they needed her to return to Cyprus. The answer was that it wasn't necessary, Barry's body, or what there was left of it, would be returned to the UK once the tests were complete and that could take another week.

Greg picked up the morning paper and noticed that the press had yet to get hold of the entire story about the grim discovery, and the quarter-column piece only confirmed the fact that not all of Barry was coming back, though, they never went into detail.

He sat next to Chrissy as Mary prepared the customary sweet tea for shock.

Chrissy drank the liquid, not once looking up from her cup. The phone rang again; it was a journalist from the Sun newspaper. The story was out and now the bandwagon would begin to roll.

Richard had browsed through dozens of website pages. He had also gone into Wikipedia, where he discovered that the Scylla was one of hundreds of sea monster legends seen or spotted all over the world, from Loch Ness to Saskatchewan.

There was even a reference to a sea monster discovered on Canvey Island in Essex, a seaside place that he had visited just once a very long time ago, when he was still in his short trousers.

He moved down the page and read the text. 'Scylla is described as a cryptid (from the Greek "κρύπτω" (krypto) meaning 'hide'), recorded in ancient texts as a monstrous form of a giant maiden in torso, with a serpent for its lower body, having six snarling dog-heads issuing from its midriff, including its twelve forelimbs.'

Richard clicked on the image he had taken at the villa and tried to enlarge it, but it was too faint for a clear view, so he went back into the search engines to look for a better one. And found it.

It was a classic mythology style painting with the scene one of carnage, as the creature depicted was ripping through a ship of mariners who had come upon it. According to other scribes of the time, the Scylla possessed more heads than they could count, and those who encountered her were killed instantly. The other chilling sentence he read gave him even more worries.

The Scylla can never be destroyed.

As he clicked from one image to the next and back to the text, the front door bell rang.

CHAPTER TWELVE

Did you miss me?

Expecting Peter had done all his research and was back early, or forgotten his key, Richard got off the sofa, made his way to the door, and opened it without looking up.

"Back already, what did you discover?" He waited for Peter to enter.

"Hello, Richard."

He stopped in his tracks and looked straight at the woman standing in front of him. "Julie! What… What are you doing here?"

"I got a call from Peter, who said you might need me. So here I am. How about a hello kiss for your wife?"

"Oh, darling, it's so good to see you. I don't believe it, what a fantastic surprise." His first stunned silence now prompted him to move forward and hold her against him, before bending down to kiss her lips passionately. God, how he had missed her and how he needed her there with him.

She opened her mouth and let her tongue kiss back. It was a long sensuous kiss, the kiss of lovers. He held her tighter, before letting go.

"Did you miss me?" Julie's eyes were bright and her face beamed a warm smile.

"Of course. But why did you come? You said you would never come here again, so why now?"

"As I mentioned, Peter rang and said you were involved in something. I thought I could be of help."

"Involved… he said that?" He looked at her closely, studying her features, as if looking for something that wasn't right, as she stood gazing at him, waiting for his next sentence.

She glanced around the room, "It's nice, cosy. He gave me the address so I just took a cab, would you like to show me around?"

He picked up her small suitcase from the floor with one hand and taking hers with the other, began the tour. "This is the lounge, the patio is through there, and the kitchen is quite big, where we spend a lot of our time, and on the front patio. The bedroom is just down here. Well, mine is. Fancy a shower after your flight?"

"Yes, good idea." Julie smiled back. "And maybe you can give me a back rub too. That's if you are not too tired, been busy I hear." She said and followed him into the bedroom.

"You could say that."

He placed the case on the floor and went into the en-suite to run the shower. The steam-jet exploded into action and the water bristled against the glass door. As he turned, he glimpsed Julie in the mirror, she had already stripped and stood naked waiting for him. His eyes lit up as he went to join her.

"I'm sure Peter won't be back for a while. We can have some private time together." She cooed and moved closer to him. Reaching for the belt on her husband's jeans, her fingers worked deftly undoing the buckle, tugging at it, and loosening it, before her right hand reached down to release the top button. His jeans popped open and her fingers slowly opened one button after another, her mouth drawing closer to his neck. Pressing her nakedness against him, his body responded to the attention.

The impromptu action of his wife's impatience created his own reaction as his passion and lust exerted itself. His arms gripped her tight as he pulled her naked body against his, pressing her breasts taut into his sweat covered shirt. Her breathing became faster, and small gasps accompanied her growing sounds of delight as her body ached for pleasure.

He couldn't wait and moved down her body to suckle on one breast. Taking the pert nipple into his mouth, he sucked gently on the bud, causing it to tremble and throb as his tongue rippled across the bare skin. He moved his mouth and hands together, alternating from one breast to the other then up to the nape of her neck to lavish kisses on her, before moving to her mouth and seeking out her tongue.

Her hands were not idle either, as she first pulled down his fast-falling jeans and then ripped away his shirt, exposing the bare chest. Her mouth began to lick and suck on it, concentrating on the erogenous zones of his body, her tongue feverishly lapping and pulling his nipples, and kissing the exposed flesh. Plying his chest hair with her fingers, she dragged them slowly across, and tightening her fingers around it, pulled gently.

Feeling the jeans at his feet, he kicked them off, just his boxers remained. She pushed them down his legs. Both stood naked, and Julie slowly slithered down the length of his body taking his aching manhood into her succulent mouth. Her tongue licking wildly, she looked up at him, caressing the flesh with her mouth, her eyes wide, and her expression one of pure wanton.

Their need as great as their passion, pulled them towards the bed, both bodies collapsing onto it. Julie spread herself open, and Richard planted kisses and more kisses on her breasts and down her stomach.

She stretched out and leaned back, all the while their mouths alternating from body to face and back again. Lips on lips as the intensity grew, keeping her mouth on his, or his tongue on her breasts, before they joined together on the bed.

His urges became more eager as his foreplay intensified. Gripping her breasts, he squeezed tighter, fondling her, and placed his hand across her stomach. Moving his hand down, he felt the heat from her body against his fingers, his stroking now causing her to tremble and her body to press tighter against his, urging him to push further into her. He felt her twist and rise then press herself against the bed, his fingers now seeking out her wetness. Her legs parted and his hand pressed against her, exposing her sex. He pushed into her with his finger, almost teasing her, before pushing another finger inside then slowly turning it first one way then the other, her body squirming and pressing and pushing against him. He closed his eyes and let the movement of his hand be his sight.

Moving up against her body, he parted her legs, and pushed himself towards her as he kissed, fondled, and teased her body, playing her emotions and senses in a symphony of pleasure and desire. Feeling his own body tighten, his arms reached under her to lift her up and guide her towards him. He opened his eyes, looked into hers, kissed her deep, and pressed his body into her.

Her mouth pressed against his and as they released, she spoke to him, "σε αγαπω,"

It was a Greek expression he knew, just one of the few he recognised, it meant, "I love you." But it also meant that the woman he was about to make love to was not his wife.

"NO," he screamed at the naked woman, her body now transformed into that of the goddess.

"You didn't know it was me? I find that difficult to believe. Does that wife of yours show you the passion I just did, does she hold you or embrace you as I do? No, you knew it was me all the time. You wanted me, and couldn't resist."

"No, never. Get out, leave me alone. I don't want you, I never have, and I wish I had never found you. I just want to be left alone." His body shook with rage and fear, knowing only too well her capabilities, and her anger now.

Still naked, she stood up and peered down at the shaking figure of the man who was crumpled on the bed. "Leave you alone? No, that is not going to happen. The next time you see me, it will be on my terms and you will plead. No… beg for me to take you. You will come on bended knee, dragging your body across the ground, ready to worship me."

"It will never happen."

"Yes, it will. I saved you once, remember? and that debt must be paid." She moved away from the bed and effortlessly past him as he lay on the bed. Her figure serene and beautiful and yet so dangerous. A goddess in all her different forms, majestic, magnificent, and malevolent.

He followed her as she glided through the passageway and out the door, which opened on its own. He wanted to chase after her but realising his nakedness, stopped at the door. The ephemeral spirit of the Goddess had gone, leaving only an indelible mark on his soul; guilt. How close he had come to making love to her was something he just couldn't put out of his mind, because somewhere right at the back of it, deep down, he wished he had.

Peter's excursion to the villa gave him a better insight into the look of the Scylla creature, but he felt it was somewhat superficial, and he still needed to learn more. As he wandered about the harbour area and up past the municipal car park, he came across an old bookshop tucked away behind one of the bars that had recently closed down.

The bar's name was obscured, the windows covered in a thick white wash, and above them hung a large FOR SALE sign in Greek and English, and a mobile number written in red across the front. Unfortunately, these signs were appearing far too often these days as businesses continued to crash.

He passed by the bar and along the narrow alley that housed the bookshop. In the window, he noticed several English, as well as Greek books. Pushing the door open, he entered.

A small Greek man dressed all in black—the usual garb of a widow or widower—greeted him. He looked old, possibly in his late seventies or early eighties, with a face so etched in memory that you could almost read the lines of his life as he looked straight at the Peter.

"Yasso, Kirio, tikanis?" Peter spoke in his best Greek.

Perhaps the man was hard of hearing or just ignorant because he didn't respond, merely reclined in the chair he was in and turned the page of his own book.

Peter was about to turn around and leave the shop when he noticed a row of books ahead of him, the sign above them written in English; Greek Mythology. He also noticed in the corner a small table and wooden chair beside it. He would find the tome he was looking for and sit there.

He picked three volumes, one of which looked modern, called 'Monsters, Myths, and Magic', a hardcover that looked rather expensive. The second was older, weather-beaten, and again in English; 'Homer's Odyssey'. Peter's first thought was what did Homer Simpson know about Greek Mythology? Then he dismissed the thought as too crass. The third was one that he opened immediately and began to read. It was called 'The Dominion of Poseidon'.

Knowing what he did of the Scylla, he scanned the index and quickly found the reference he was searching for. As he sat down in the chair, he looked over to the old man at the counter, who, mysteriously, was nowhere to be seen. Peter started reading quickly, making notes as he went.

The main story seemed to emanate from Greece, where Scylla, the daughter of Craetis, was one of two sea monsters in mythology, the other being Charybdis. Both lived on opposite sides of a narrow channel of water within an arrow's range of each other; the space between them within touching distance, so that sailors attempting to avoid Charybdis, would pass too close to

Scylla, and vice versa. Hence, the origin of the phrase between 'a rock and a hard place'. The strait has long been associated with the Strait of Messina, between Italy and Sicily, but more recently, the theory has been challenged and the alternative location of Cape Skilla in North West Greece suggested. She was one of the children of Phorcys and Ceto, known as the Phorcydes.

He studied the picture; she had the face and torso of a woman and below, six dog heads grew from her stomach, supported by twelve canine legs, and some form of a fish's tail. He found a small writing pad and began scribbling furiously as he browsed through the pages. He grabbed a heavy book and checked the contents; finding earlier references to the Scylla made in Homer's Odyssey, Book 12, and this particular one confirmed the legend as he read the words.

'She's not human, but a destroyer who will never die, fearful, difficult, and fierce, not someone you can fight. There's no defence against her. The bravest thing to do is run away. If you linger by the cliff to arm yourself, I fear she'll jump out once more, attack you with all her heads and snatch away six men, just as before. Row on quickly past her, as hard as you can go.' Homer, Odyssey, Book 12

He read it through again slowly. From the sound of it, The Scylla was not something to be messed with, myth or not. Sitting back, he picked up the final tome next to him, 'Monsters, Myths, and Magic'. He thumbed through the pages, they all seemed to be there. Medusa, The Hydra, The Minotaur, Harpies, The Kraken, and The Scylla, whose picture was particularly graphic and was captured so expertly by illustrator Philip Prendergast, who definitely had a great style when it came to monsters.

The price of this particular book was expensive; at forty-five Euros, it was a lot to pay for an imaginary friend. He closed it and went back to his notes. As he read the passage again, one phrase stood out, *'If you linger by the cliff to arm yourself, I fear she will jump out once more.'*

The cliff part seemed to ring a bell and he thought for a second, *'the missing English tourist, whose body part they found recently was at a cliff. Surely he couldn't have...'* He paused, holding the idea. "No, that's impossible. I'm getting as bad as Richard now."

He shut the books and made his way gingerly back towards where the old man had been sitting, but was nowhere to be seen. He placed the books on the counter, walked away, and didn't look back.

Emerging from behind the counter of the shop, the old man's first words were, "Πιστεύετε ότι βρήκατε αυτό δεν διαψεύστηκε." Directed at the immaculately dressed Mr Christoulides, who came from the back and approached him.

With a sly smile on his face, as if his plans were coming together as he intended, Mr Christoulides said. "επίρ. ίσως, πιθανόν." His affirmation of Peter's visit indicating that he was more than a silent partner in this adventure.

Richard dressed quickly. His last encounter with the goddess had left him naked and breathless as he tried to chase after her. How did he ever think that he could catch her? She was not of this world, or any he knew. But her words were the thing that haunted him most, far more than her ghostly appearance. For they issued an ultimatum, one that he could not ignore. As he sat on the sofa, he feared for the consequences of his second rebuke of her. Needing to be sure that nothing had happened to his family, he picked up Peter's house phone and dialled Julie. He needed to talk to her; needed to hear her voice.

The connection seemed to take ages as he waited for the ring tone, once, twice, three times.

"Hello," Julie never said the number, something she had picked up from watching too many phone movies and it stayed with her.

"Hi, Jules." He waited for her next sentence.

"Hi, Hun, I got your message, but sorry, been out shopping. Lots to do, Simon is coming for dinner this weekend, so I thought I'd better get some stuff in; chicken, nothing too fancy with the usual crop of veggies. You okay?"

Julie's knack for multi-tasking conversations was an annoyance, but today, he didn't care, he just wanted to hear her voice. Just needed to know she was safe.

"I'm fine. Just thought I'd call you. Also been busy, trying to sort out things." He could almost see her as he spoke.

She would have three things in her hands, balancing the phone under her chin whilst propped up against the side of her head. Their talk was normal, nothing other than a husband and wife discussing their day. But for him it was much more than that, it meant nothing had happened to her, or the kids. At least, not yet. His heart had stopped pounding, had been in overdrive ever since the goddess left, but with Julie's words, it had calmed down.

"I hope to be back next week; the courts should be all done by then." He hesitated before he spoke next. "I don't suppose you want to come over?"

"No, thanks. Why, do you want me there then?" She paused. "You are not in any trouble, are you?"

Why did he ask if she wanted to come over? That was stupid. Because now he had planted the seed of doubt and for both their sakes he had better quell her suspicions quickly. "No. It's just that the weather is really good at the moment, and I thought you might enjoy a few days in the sun, once the court case is over." He had rescued it, but only just.

"No, I'm fine, and I've had enough Cyprus sun to last me for a couple of years. Thanks, anyway. I got to go, stuff to do and the fish I bought for tonight needs to get cooked; fish on Fridays. Call me later, okay? Tomorrow, or Sunday. Bye, love." She ended the conversation, without giving him another chance to reply.

He leaned back with the phone next to him, the time and date showing on the screen.

Peter's car pulled into the driveway.

CHAPTER THIRTEEN

I warned you

Aphrodite returned to her lair, her next move clear, and ready for implementing.

"I told you your power was weak, Father. You could not stop me from seeing him and will not stop me from destroying him. No man or god refuses me twice. I shall make him suffer and he shall regret his act. Do you hear me, Father, do you hear me?" Her ranting cries rang out across her rock cave sanctuary.

The echoes of the sea and the waves ebbed and flowed, hitting the ragged rocks below her, creating the age-old symphony of time and circumstance, reflected down through the eons and forged into the craggy time eroded rocks.

Aphrodite's face was one of anger, retribution her motivation, and inspiration.

She would exact a revenge that would make those around her tremble, and in doing so regain her status as a revered and feared goddess.

She moved from her throne of stone, down the steps carved out in the cave to the floor below to summon her servant. She stretched out her hand across the water and the foam from whence she came, bubbled, creating small eddies that whirled and whisked into little pillars of froth, rising upwards off the waves.

From the foam-filled turrets of water the first sight of the Scylla appeared, as it broke from the depths to the surface, to greet her.

The creature's body was heavy and thickset with horned and scaly skin, her limbs twisting like vipers, snaking, and curling under her form. Her fleshy scarlet torso gaped open like a wound, exposing the snarling snapping heads of the six canines as they met the goddess with howls of obedience.

But as grotesque as the body of this demon was, her face looked as if beatified, its loveliness beyond compare, with auburn hair in glowing tresses that draped across her naked shoulders, her eyes a brilliant emerald green that glistened and shimmered; her cheeks and mouth a fleshy shade of alabaster, with skin soft, smooth, and perfect.

Aphrodite stepped forward to welcome her.

The Scylla lowered her head in tribute as she floated gently on the waves.

"We have one more task to do, my sister." Aphrodite moved closer to the water's edge and Scylla listened. "After this, Mr. Cole will find it difficult. No, I would say impossible to ignore, and not comply with."

No more words were necessary, the conversation becoming almost telepathic, as if the Scylla knew just what she wanted. Then finally acknowledging the goddess with a flick of her tail before sinking back into the waves, the last vestiges of her tail-like tentacles flapped the water and created a large splash, the swell from her body edging towards the rocky shore.

Since Peter's return, he and Richard had spent the past hour mulling over the information they had collected. The irony was that even though Peter didn't really believe the story, he was enjoying the search and the adventure.

Richard had a way of getting to him that other people didn't, and Peter knew that playing along was the best way for them both. Besides, he was having a grand time of it. He related his tale of the villa, finding the cosy bookshop, and showed him his hurriedly scribbled notes. So together, and with the help of the internet, they could learn a great deal more about their adversary.

Both sat at the table as the printer churned out another page of references.

"What do we know so far?" Richard's question was poised at concrete answers.

"We know she is one mean fucker, that's for sure." Peter's lewd comment was all the more pertinent as he held in his hand one of the graphic images of the Scylla he had collected from the web. "And according to Homer, and a few others of that age, she can't be killed. So, we are off to a good start."

"Definitely." Richard sat back in the chair, picked up another picture, and stared at it for a few seconds.

"Of course, the most troubling thing of all is…" Peter paused, not sure if he should say it.

"What's that?"

"She doesn't exist." Peter felt compelled to blurt it out, but in doing so, he broke the momentum of their search. He brought it all back to reality, and how.

"Don't you think I know that?" Richard desperately wanted to tell him of his meeting with the goddess and her planned seduction, but couldn't. Peter's faith in him, or what was left of it, would be gone the moment he disclosed such an unbelievable encounter. So, in the meantime, he had to humour him to get him back on his side. But perhaps if he explained his thoughts a bit more, it might help clarify things. He fished around in his head to find some idea or some reasoning behind his quest. "I totally agree with you. Reality tells us that creatures like this don't exist; she is up there with Ghosts, Spirits, UFO's, Bigfoot, and yes, other Sea

Monsters. Yet, people still believe in them, like they believe in God or Angels or the Devil. They exist because we want them to.

"We as humans like to cling to something that is beyond our imagination, something that is extraordinary, and we look to these paranormal happenings to validate our existence, regardless of what they are. For our purpose, our particular phenomenon is this creature. True, all reason tells me it doesn't exist, but what if my rationality is wrong and beings like this do live, not in our reality, but for some reason cross over from their world to ours? Isn't that worth finding out about? I believe we must delve into these things. It's in our nature to look for the impossible. Just because we can't see it, doesn't mean it isn't there. What lives in the dark, lives in the dark, we just can't see it, but it's still there. I know it's difficult to comprehend, but we need an open-mind. We must consider the possibility. And that's all I need you to do, consider the possibility."

Peter sat looking at him then glanced at the papers spread out across the table. Many of the images were familiar, some were not, but all contained some element of the supernatural in one shape or another, be it mythical monster or modern-day camera shot. He picked up the Scylla picture and examined it, more than he had done before. "Given that this," he pointed. "Is what we have to find… Do you have any idea how we are going to do that?" He pushed the image towards Richard.

"No, but I think I know someone who might."

"And who would that be?"

"Mr. Christoulides. He said he would help when the time was right. Well, I don't think there is a better time than now." Richard passed the paper back.

"If you can't find him, how are you going to find that?"

"I don't think I have to, he finds me."

"You think so? Tell you what, the next time you arrange to meet him I'm coming too, because I really want to see this man of mystery." Peter picked up the image of the Scylla again. "She really is some ugly Mother. Just listen to this.

" 'It's true her voice sounds like a new-born pup, but she's a vicious monster. Nobody would feel good seeing her, nor would a god who crossed her path. She has a dozen feet, all deformed, six enormously long necks, with a horrific head on each of them and three rows of teeth packed close together full of murky death. ' Charming, isn't she?"

"I warned you. Once we get started on this who knows where it might lead?"

"Yes, well, just as long as we don't meet this thing in the dark, that's fine with me."

"I'm sure when the time comes, if it does, we will both be ready." Richard sighed, knowing he had won back his friend, who was now on his side.

Paphos, Saturday night

It was time to leave the villa, and both opted to spend the evening in Paphos. To have a quiet drink away from the tourist area. Somewhere where they could relax, take in the view, just chill, and forget about things. In town, they found the perfect place, *the 5th Floor*. It was not expensive or vastly elaborate but it had a great view across town, with small tables and sofas set on the outside of a small dining area.

The food was international, with a choice of menu. Peter settled for a pork chop with French fries, and a Greek salad, whilst Richard went for his customary cheeseburger and chips. Crowned off with two large Carlsbergs to wash it down with.

The camaraderie had returned to their exchanges, both enjoying each other's company, even if perhaps for different reasons. Throughout the evening, they didn't talk about the quest, conversation staying mainly focused on their wives, or in Peter's case, the lack of one. Around them, the restaurant was doing good business, as the younger generation began to take over.

CHAPTER FOURTEEN

For those in Peril on the Sea

Ayia Napa, Nisi Beach, Sunday morning
It was odd to see a Papas, the Greek name for a Priest, on the shores of Nisi Beach dressed in his long black robe, which hung from his body like a human curtain. With no shape to the garment or design, it was just one long piece of cloth that covered him, his only other adornment a solid Greek cross, possibly gold, which occasionally caught the sun and sent mini flashes across the morning shadows.

His demeanour and the way he walked with stooped shoulders and a heavy tread belied his age. He was no more than fifty but looked considerably older, with the customary black heavy-set beard, brown eyes, and a wizened brow just about visible. He carried with him a small incense burner, which was already lit and now wafted its fumes across the shore as he swung it back and forth and from side to side, repeating an incantation that seemed only for his ears.

The select group watching the ceremony were especially chosen to represent, not just the community, but also some of the local trade's people. Solidarity in sorrow; that was what the municipality was going for, and it was working.

At the front of the group stood Heracles Aristides, next to him, Panayotis Linos, Christina Skalos, Francoise Mulot, and Gregor Tabachi. The two Greek men were dressed in black suits and black shirts, with no ties, as was the custom for funerals and memorials. The women wore mid-length black skirts and white blouses buttoned up to the neck, with sensible flat shoes, as the beach was no place for heels.

The Russian wore a black sports jacket, and trousers, and a pair of what looked like patented Churchill-style black shoes. The one difference between him and the other two men was that he wore a white shirt and black tie, done in a full Windsor knot, and his hair was gelled. He looked very solemn and dignified, as they all did.

The priest returned from the water's edge and addressed the gathering. He read out Barry's name and that of Nilu Comaneci, the young Romanian boy, who had also been lost at sea, as he would at the Greek service of Μνημόσυνα, (mnemosyna), though, strictly speaking, this wasn't one of those, as the deceased weren't Greek Orthodox or even buried yet. There were however two Μνημόσυνα, taking place at that time, one in Nicosia and the other in Orounta.

The Papas broke into a few words of English with a heavy Cypriot lilt on each. "We shall sing a tune now, for the dead." His sentence sounded somewhat severe but probably was the best English phrase he knew for the occasion.

One sheet of photocopied paper was quickly handed out to those who had gathered. A small group of British tourists stood slightly away from the main body at the top of the beach road, where the Kelly family also was, at the back. Three or four other families joined the proceedings.

The Kellys' two kids had no clue what was going on, and all they wanted was to be back in the pool at the apartment block, the beach the last place for them right now. How long it would take before Josh went back in the ocean, was anyone's guess. But they wanted, no, needed, to show their respect. Even for them, the choice of tune seemed a little odd, but perhaps it was the only English hymn the municipality knew that had any reference to the sea. Under the circumstances it seemed almost comic, as the first strains of the disjointed song began and people tried to sing along.

"For those in peril on the Sea…" The singing at best, was audible, but tuneful, no.

Off to the right of the assembly, one woman stood silently, Rita Comaneci. In one hand, she clutched a picture of her son, and in the other a small bunch of white roses; tears rolled slowly down her cheeks, her eyes misted with more tears as she stared lifelessly towards the horizon. Then looking down at the picture, she placed it into the bunch of roses, and made her way down to the shore just as the singing stopped.

Larnaca

Jenny Speagel had sat on the wooden bench seat for half an hour. Larnaca police station was busy. There had been some disturbances late in the night and they had made for a busy time for the force. Jenny sat alongside two other possible customers, one looked Eastern European, and spent most of his time scanning a book and twitching his fingers, which were nicotine stained, a habit she despised, though today, she felt she could be tempted to light up. Her nerves were in tatters.

Lenny had been missing for three days and this was her last chance saloon. She knew she had to report his disappearance, much as she hated doing it, because she feared there could be questions she preferred not to answer; once she sat down with them, and she knew exactly the type of questions they would ask.

"Did he do this before, gone off on his own? Was he having an affair? Was he involved in something illegal? He had a boat, did he use it for illicit purposes?" That incriminating last line of questioning was the one she feared the most.

In the dark depths, the Scylla lurked in the bottomless caves off the south-east coast of the island, which had now become her new home. Not risking returning to the Zenobia, she skulked in the shadows, her presence undetectable either by eye, ear, or sonar. As large and foreboding as she was, the massive caves offered her sanctuary, until needed again.

CHAPTER FIFTEEN

Till death do us part?

Paphos, Midday

The wedding business is big in Cyprus, with Aphrodite's Island being selected as one of the most romantic destinations on the planet. But with the disappearance of the Rocks at Petra Tou Romiou, the site had lost some of its appeal with newlyweds. Nevertheless, many young wedded couples still took to the shore to have their pictures taken at the place where the Goddess of Love came from the foam, before embarking on their wedding celebrations.

In recent years, the harbour of Paphos has become like a wedding parade, as new brides and grooms, and their families and guests descend upon it for their nuptials, most of which are sea-faring ones, taken aboard a variety of craft, from small yachts and ocean cruisers, to pirate ships and catamarans.

How lavish the wedding breakfast and entertainment is comes down to budget. And that was certainly the case for Gary and Hazel Connelly, who had chosen Cyprus as the place they wanted to get married in, as Hazel had once been a tour operator's representative and knew the island well. She was also able to bend a few ears to get some cheap deals for accommodation for her entourage, as well as the festivities she had planned.

Hazel's and Gary's wedding was a civil ceremony, small but intimate, and conducted by the municipality, with just a few close friends in attendance. It was in complete contrast to a traditional Greek wedding, where five-hundred plus or the entire village, is often the turn out.

Like all brides, Hazel looked beautiful, her white satin gown decorated with a motif of lace and pearls shimmering in the bright sunlight, the tight corset she wore underneath keeping her six-week pregnancy bump secret.

With the ceremony over, the couple and guests posed for a few photographs before the wedding vehicles arrived to take them to the harbour. As they set off accompanied by a fanfare of car horns from guests and strangers alike, the brightest smile appeared on Hazel's face. Whatever the future held for either of them, they would see it through together.

Hazel held her new husband's hand and kissed him lovingly on his lips. The "Just Married" sign on the back of the car fell off as they turned sharp left at the lights down to the harbour.

The wedding party arrived at the dock, and the four or five cars soon joined, accompanied by a large double-decker London bus, which looked completely out-of-place in the small Paphos pedestrian thoroughfare as it unloaded its passengers, who were all dressed in their finest attire. The twenty or so invited guests, busied themselves into small groups, snapping pictures and knocking back bottles of wine and beer that seemed locked in most of the guests' hands.

Congregating behind the wedded couple, the colourful group set off to board the wedding boat. They passed several restaurants and waved to the diners, who in turn smiled and waved back, wishing them 'Good Luck' in a variety of languages as they tucked into their meals.

The newlyweds moved towards the castle area and the gang-plank at the end of the pier and gingerly stepped aboard the boat aptly named, *Chastity*, which was appropriately decorated with hundreds of pink and white balloons framing its sides.

The dining area was also arrayed with a full silver service and in the centre, was a three-tier wedding cake, especially bought and paid for by Hazel's work colleagues, who had flown across with the couple.

Gary's Mother sat beside Hazel and her Matron of Honour, Ellen, as Gary's best man, Alan, began to point people in the right direction, even though their names were on place cards and everyone could find their own seats. In between pointing, Alan took large sips of red wine, which were mixed with his already consumed two glasses of scotch and two pints of Carlsberg. Alan was just a tad nervous.

The *Chastity* sounded its horn, as it set sail away from the harbour, en-route to Larnaca. It would take four hours or more for the journey, as no one was in a hurry. Hazel had especially charted this vessel as she knew it and the owners well, having brought hundreds of passengers to them during the time she was in Cyprus.

The crew and waiters went about their tasks mechanically, all having done this a hundred, perhaps even a thousand times before. Although every wedding or celebration was slightly different, it was still easy to become complacent, look bored, and turn surly. But in Hazel's case, knowing her well, they did none of this, taking their tasks with great enthusiasm and commitment, chatting to the guests, making sure they were well catered for, and attended to.

The food being served was a mix of Greek and International dishes with a few extras added such as Cauliflower Cheese, Hazel's favourite, and for Gary, a couple of Yorkshire puddings, which he had brought over for the occasion. Of course, he could have bought them from most supermarkets in Cyprus, but he wanted to be sure that he got them and they were on his plate.

As the boat left the harbour, the sea grew slightly choppier. With the bow heading into open water, the sway increased and the waves buffeted the bow. Inside, the festivities were well underway and voices rose in volume as the breakfast began to take on a party mood, with speeches and Champagne being readied. Hazel and Gary had been selective with their guest list, because although both had hundreds of relatives, they invited a chosen few to celebrate their nuptials, so only those who could afford the flight came.

One couple, Steve and Naomi, brought their kids, twins Ricky and Pixie, aged six, who had spent most of the wedding breakfast crawling from one table to the next and getting under the feet of guests. And when they weren't doing that, they were trying to get at one of the pink balloons that hung at the back of the cake table. It was left to Gary's Uncle Fabian, well in his fifties and with a heart condition—fortunately now under control—to rescue the situation and plonk the kids back at the table where their parents sat. A somewhat embarrassed and annoyed Steve and Naomi nodded politely at the return of their offspring.

Out in open water, the *Chastity* began to pick up speed and bumped its way through the waves washing over its bows. The wedding breakfast was fast approaching its conclusion and it was time for speeches.

Gary stood first, pushing his dessert plate aside and picking up a champagne glass. Hazel had just the one bridesmaid, Ellen, her Matron of Honour, so Gary was going to let Alan toast her. Gary had just to thank everybody for turning up and then leave the main show to Alan. He put the glass down and rifled through his pockets for his speech. He checked two, it was not there, then he remembered putting it inside his jacket pocket.

Taking it out, he folded the paper over, placed it on the table, and waited.

The boat moved sharply to the left, which brought forth a loud 'whoa' from the assembly. Before it corrected its course and slowed down, Gary sat down quickly and stood up again even quicker.

The boat began slowing down again, the engines churned and vibrated, and the bridge began to receive signals from its instruments panel that made no sense and instigated the boat's reduction in speed.

"Dearly beloved... Oh, no, we did that earlier."

His joke was well received as the congregation broke into a short applause.

The boat lurched again, this time more violently, and the tables slid precariously from one side to the other, followed by two loud muffled embarrassed shrieks across the room, before a second heavier thump and what seemed like a long deep scratching sound underneath the hull accompanied the next sharp movement. The screams grew more in number and louder in volume, as frightened people began to react to the noise coming from below.

There was silence for a few seconds; an alarmed, pensive hush that pierced the atmosphere, as the noise subsided, and the boat steadied. A sense of relief manifested itself across the passengers' faces before a second eerie sound of more scraping against the bottom interrupted the mood and the calm on the *Chastity*. Then, it began to rock slowly from side to side, before becoming faster and faster, as the grating and scratching grew louder and the swaying more violent as if the vessel was being pulled and shaken from underneath.

The wedding cake teetered on the edge of the table where Uncle Fabian stood sentry, as if protecting it, then it collapsed, as the boat shifted violently, first one way, then the other, as if being dragged along, before the deck began to rise upwards, spilling the people like skittles across the floor.

Hazel fell, and reached out to grab her husband, her beautiful white dress coated in the remnants of the wedding breakfast. Screaming voices joined the roaring sounds of the boat's engines as they whirled and blistered, sending shards of metal from below deck into the mêlée of people now clinging to life in the dining room.

The floor cracked, then cracked again, the floorboards snapped one by one as a huge opening appeared, and sea water gushed into the craft through holes that were rapidly appearing across the deck, sucking guests through the gaping fissures of the fractured and broken hull. The passengers' terrified cries were also soon quaffed by the surging water, which filled their mouths and throats as they gasped for air. As the sea continued to swell and pour in, its suction pulling the bodies down into the swirling maelstrom.

The *Chastity's* horn and sirens wailed out across a deserted and silent horizon, with no other craft in sight able to react or hear as she fought for life. For with each second she fought, she rose higher in the water. As wood and metal splintered, electrics collapsed, sending fresh sparks and flames shooting indiscriminately across the fragmented deck, snapping sparks at the helm, as orange and scarlet fingers of flames began rising higher and higher bonded by thick black smoke, which hovered over the stricken vessel.

The people inside, crew and passengers alike, clung to whatever they could find. Gary had his arm wrapped around a service pipe disguised behind the wall, and clinging to his trousers' belt was Hazel, her hold waning as her fingers began to lose their grip. She tried to push herself higher onto him, to grab him tighter, but as she did, another vicious wrench of the vessel released her hand and separated them, her last words of "I love you," lost in the crescendo of a dying ship's last breath as she plunged down across the floor, into the broken hull, and into the sea.

From his last vantage point at the top of the helm, Captain Takis tried calling on his cell phone, knowing the boat's radio and all other communications had gone. But there was no signal and no one could hear them. No 'May Day' distress call would ever be heard.

The *Chastity* began to bottom out, as a vast explosion ripped through her belly, which enveloped the damaged carcass of the failing boat now engulfed by flames and dense smoke.

Captain Takis grappled with the last lifebelt to release it before the ship lurched, and pulled himself higher onto the roof of his bridge. He looked down into the depths, and noticed a mysterious shape lying under the water. He could not make it out or be certain but it looked animal in origin. He tried to reach his camera button on his mobile phone but the boat began to sink fast and as he tried to grab a railing, he lost his footing and crashed down into the gaping hole that beckoned him.

Those passengers who could, emptied into the oil coated sea, gurgling and swallowing, choking from the smoke and oily water as the *Chastity* ungraciously gave way to her agony, and began to sink into the depths.

The sparsely dotted life-craft and lifebelts bobbled in the waves, amidst some floating debris, tempting the terrified people in the water to grab onto whatever they could to save themselves.

The attack complete, the Scylla sank back into the depths, her job done.

"Now, we shall see what happens, Mr. Cole. We shall see." Aphrodite's words rang out across the empty cave, her plan in action.

CHAPTER SIXTEEN

What do we do now?

Ayia Napa, afternoon

Mr Heracles had decided that the offer of lunch for the Kellys and Mrs Comaneci was not the best course of action under the circumstances, he felt instead, it was better to allow them the time and space they needed. Of course, he would be making himself and his team available if called upon at any time, but lunch, no, that would be a little too crass on this particular day. This was the message Panayotis was to deliver to Mrs Comaneci and the Kellys.

Panayotis had felt a certain trepidation as he walked over to the Kellys, and spoke briefly to them, before turning his attention to Mrs Comaneci, whom he had seen earlier go down to the shore, but now she was not around.

'Perhaps that's for the best,' he thought as he walked back to his imposing Black Mercedes, the usual mode of transport for men of standing on the island. He was about to leave the parking area when Christina came running over to him.

She looked dishevelled, the top buttons on her blouse had popped open, and her bra showed.

Panayotis tried to avoid looking at her cleavage as she bent down to speak to him through the open window.

"It has happened again…" She was breathless from running, as it was something alien to her, but the panic in her voice could not be ignored.

Panayotis sat in the car waiting for her next sentence.

"Only this time, it's a boat! A fucking boat." She took a deep breath. "A wedding boat from Paphos." Her chest heaved as her words carried to Panayotis' ears.

He had guessed there would be another attack, or another incident, he just didn't know where, when, or what. "Slow down, Christina, and tell me again, slowly. Take your time; just get your breath back." He leaned out of the car window and took her hand, steadying her as she tried to deliver the same speech again.

Christina, regaining some of her composure, stood almost at attention as she brushed herself down, and returned the popped buttons to their button-holes, her cleavage now hidden. She spoke again, this time much calmer. "Panayotis, sorry… I just found out that somewhere off Larnaca, a boat has blown up. There are a few survivors that I know of, but no actual figures for sure. It seems the boat just sank and no one knows why. They have sent people out to investigate, police, even a few army, navy personnel, and the coast guard. A helicopter is flying over the scene. That is the last I heard."

"When?" Panayotis needed answers.

"Not sure exactly, I just know that the boat was carrying a wedding party."

"What boat, how big, how many passengers, where was it headed?" All Panayotis' questions needed answering but she was not the best one for that right now. He needed to know facts, and fast.

"I don't know, I don't have that information yet." Christina's frustration was all too evident.

"I will drive to Larnaca and see what I can find out. Tell the police I am coming."

"Okay, I will call them now." She turned and walked quickly back to her own car, opened the door, and picked up her cell phone. She found the number and called while watching Panayotis' car slam into reverse and the tyres, which had never skidded before, left a long black mark across the concrete, as he sped from the car park and down the beach road.

Paphos, afternoon

Most of the day had been spent sifting through the information they had gathered from websites, even finding references to the Ayia Napa monster on a TV show called 'Destination Truth', which had been submitted through You Tube. The crew coming to Cyprus in search of the famed sea monster, 'To Filiko Teras'.

Both knew that the monster they were looking for was not the cryptid known to the locals as the 'Friendly Monster', which the TV team had set out to investigate. This one was described as more like a serpent in shape, and substantially smaller than the Scylla. Still, it conveyed an air of mystique that all good legends portrayed, and made for good TV and copy.

As they browsed the images and text spread out before them, Peter went to the kitchen and returned with coffee and some forgotten cold toasted Halloumi and Lounza sandwiches. "Let's take a break, we have been at this for hours."

"I shall call Julie in a while, Simon and his family have gone for lunch today. See how that went."

"Is your brother like you?" He didn't know much about Richard's family, so now was as good a time as any to ask.

"No, not really, he's more level-headed than me, always has been. He's the type of guy who wears a coat and takes a brolly out with him, even when the sun shines, just in case it rains. I'd say he's over-cautious, protective even."

"Not a bad thing to be cautious."

"Yes, but I wish he would take a risk or two sometimes."

"Like you?"

The comment sat just a little prickly on Richard's conscience. "Hmm, point taken." He bit into his sandwich, and even though it was cold, the delicious mix of Lounza and grilled Halloumi was always a treat for his taste buds. He picked up his still warm coffee.

Peter reached for the remote to turn on the TV. The volume on the set was down and the station broadcasting was Rik 1.

Disturbing pictures flashed across the screen without sound. The scene unfolding before them seeming all the more troubling as it was the rescue of the *Chastity* passengers. A text message ran across the bottom of the screen in Greek, but some of the words were picked out in English.

Peter exchanged a glance with Richard; both knew what the other was thinking.

Larnaca, same day

The Larnaca police station was overcrowded with media and police officers, all mingled together in the hallway, the commotion was obvious as they all seemed to be waiting for the arrival of someone important. The noise grew louder as more information started to filter its way through the station. Jenny Speagel sat, still waiting, but started to eavesdrop on what was going on. As far as she could make out there has been an attack on a boat. She tried nudging herself closer to the centre of the conversation to learn a little more.

She was already on her third coffee, which she promptly put down under the chair she was seated at.

The motley assortment of magazines had already been read from cover to cover and lay strewn on the table.

She had already been up to the reception area five times, always with the same question. "How much longer will it be?" Now, she had another question. Would she get the same answer as before, just another shrug of the shoulders? She would never know because as she stood up to walk over, the door burst open and chaos ensued.

Panayotis pushed through the crowd and into the hallway where Jenny stood and fired questions at some of the officers at the same time as the media fired them at him. Communications were all in Greek, which Jenny listened to and translated in her head.

"A wedding boat just sunk off Larnaca, there are survivors but no one knows how many yet, or how many fatalities. The boat sailed from Paphos, carrying a wedding party."

Flashing cameras and raised microphones, with logos of most of the Cypriot broadcasters stuck on the end of them were thrust towards Panayotis, so he was broadcasting across the networks.

Jenny pushed her way through the people and spoke above the voices. 'Ο σύζυγός μου λείπει το σκάφος βυθίστηκε πάρα πολύ.' She hoped she had said. "My husband is also missing, his boat sank too."

The group turned to Jenny; a police officer grabbed her arm and pushed her away.

Panayotis remonstrated with the policeman, pulled Jenny from the man, and said. "σταματώ, εμποδίζω."

He eased her away from the pack of police and media and ushered her into a room off the hallway. Poking his head just a fraction out the door, he issued instructions not to be disturbed then closed it behind him.

Jenny stood and waited for him to speak to her.

"Please, sit. I'm Panayotis Linos, I work for the government and I would like to know more about your husband's disappearance. Please, sit."

"Thank you." She gazed into the man's eyes, and saw two elements, concern and curiosity. That semblance was bringing her around to trusting him, but she still needed to be cautious with her answers. "I'm Jenny Speagal and my husband disappeared three days ago. We run a small diving school and have a licence to dive at the Zenobia wreck. I think he went back there, because that's the last place we were diving at."

"I see. But why do you think he went back? Did something go wrong the last time you were there to warrant his return to the wreck?" He began to write notes on a piece of paper he snatched from the desk.

"I think it's because I saw something that frightened me… and now he's missing." Her stomach felt like a scrunched-up paper bag, and she was unsure if she could relive those moments again. But for Lenny, she had to. Because, unexpectedly and in a bizarre kind of way, things were beginning to make sense. What she had seen was a mere prelude to the current mayhem. Lenny had gone to fix it, and now she was certain, he too came upon the thing on the ship. "I apologise for my rattled nerves, but may I have a glass of water?" She needed something to settle her.

Panayotis poured a plastic cup of ice cold water from the dispenser. "You said your husband's boat is lost as well? Tell me why you think that?"

"Mr…"

"Panayotis."

"Mr Panayotis, what I am about to tell you is as hard for me to repeat as it may be for you to believe, but, it happened. We took a group of divers to the Zenobia a few days ago. Usually, I stay on board with the newbies, but that day they were all capable so I went with them. I know the wreck quite well so I decided to explore. From the word go there was something odd about the ship.

Most wrecks make noises but she was extremely quiet, just the odd creak or rattle. I started looking around and found an old Swedish Kroner under one of the grills.

"As I picked it up a shadowy shape moved in the gloom. I could not make it out, and against my better judgement, I decided to follow. I turned on my torch and began to chase this thing through the decks. I didn't have a lot of air in the tank so I knew I couldn't go too far, but the excitement had taken me over and I kept going. Then I stopped, I was in a place I didn't recognise. All I could hear were the bubbles from my tank and my heart racing. I pushed this door, which was jammed but I managed to get open, and looked down. I felt a rush of water surge past me, as if one of the ship's holds had opened.

"It was then I saw them. First, they were like two stationary red dots and I thought they might be lights left on a machine, but then they started moving towards me. I stepped back and the dots got bigger and bigger as they came closer and closer. I wasn't really thinking but intuitively, I shone the torch straight at them. They were eyes, huge red eyes, and I couldn't stop myself from staring at them. If I could have screamed I would have but there was no voice in me, all I felt was sheer terror as those eyes got closer.

"Alarmed, I dropped the torch, and tried to push my way out of the door, which was stuck, and I started to panic. But as the torch hit the bottom, the beam flashed upward in an arc and it startled the thing, and within seconds, the eyes were gone. I squeezed through the door and swam as fast as I could to the surface.

"Lenny, who was on the seabed, saw me swimming and must have realised something was amiss, because he also made his way to the surface. The others dragged me on board as I openly wept and my body shook. I begged Lenny to never go back there, but it was our livelihood…

I think what attacked the boat today is the same thing that took my Lenny. I'm sure he returned to find it, and kill it, but never came back. I did go look for him but it was getting dark by the time I got there and couldn't see anything, or the boat anywhere. Boats don't just disappear on water, unless they are sunk."

"So, you think that what you saw is the cause of these attacks?"

"I'm sure of it because there is no other explanation for what is going on. There is something in the waters killing people, and I know I saw it. That is what destroyed the wedding boat today. Surely, you can see the connection."

"I can see this is most upsetting, but the only connection I can make right now is with the press and this accident today. A sea monster in Larnaca or Paphos is just too fantastic a tale to believe, even if we have the myth in Ayia Napa about the cryptid 'Filiko Teras', our local Friendly Monster, and no doubt, you are aware of this yourself. Look, I am not saying you did not see something that frightened you, but you can appreciate that what you just told me is difficult to comprehend. Honestly, I would never venture to that wreck, and I know that when you start to lose air all sorts of images and hallucinations can materialize. I think your mind was playing tricks on you, that's all, nothing to worry about. I'm sure your husband is safe too, and doubtless, he's just messing about somewhere."

Jenny found it hard to control her temper let alone cope with the man's arrogance. "Where is my husband then, and the boat?"

"Be assured, we will look for him, and if I hear anything, I will let you know. And you do the same. Here is my card, call me anytime and keep in touch, I'm sure he'll turn up soon. I will make sure the police have a report and follow it up. Let me see you out." Panayotis took her hand, led her to the door, and opening it, followed her out.

She took the card and barged past the posse of press crowded around. As she walked down the corridor and into the hallway, she had already forgotten his name. She also knew her next move was to get off the island as fast as possible, because Lenny was not coming back.

"What do we do now?" Peter's question posed many others.

None of which Richard had replies for. "I haven't a clue." He drank what was left of the coffee, and stared blankly at the TV as images of the *Chastity* disaster began to repeat themselves. "I'm going for a walk." He said and got off the sofa, his face drained of colour. He needed fresh air, needed to be out in the open.

"You want me to come with you?"

"No, I'm fine, thanks. Just need to clear my head and figure out what to do next. Keep an eye on the TV, see what happens."

"Sure. But if you need me, call, okay?"

Richard nodded, picked up his cell phone, walked out onto the patio, down the stairs, and into the street. The late afternoon sun was still quite warm, as he picked up his pace and moved towards the beach area around Kato Pafos.

Most of the beaches were busy with tourists but some small areas were not occupied. He made his way to a minor inlet where he could look out to sea. As he sat down on the stones, they left a damp patch on his jeans. The breeze passed over him like a warm hand touching his face and he closed his eyes.

"Mr Cole, the time is very close."

He snapped his eyes open. Standing before him in the sunlight was Lukas Christoulides.

"I wondered when you'd turn up, you always seem to know where I'm going to be."

"I have my spies. But no matter, because for now it is a question of what do you do? As you can see, she has left you little doubt that she will not stop until she has you in her grasp. It is for you to decide how many more will suffer before you make the decision to obey her, cruel as it may be."

"I have already decided; this last episode with the boat was the deal-breaker. Killing innocent people on a whim is murder in any one's language." He looked straight at Lukas.

"Yes, it is, but she sees it as necessary, a means to an end. The end being yours. I fear if you do not capitulate now you will see her turn her attentions to a more personal target, one closer to home. You do understand my meaning?"

"Yes, I realise that all too well."

"I am afraid her power and her will are strong now and she controls your destiny much more than you do. She could show compassion and mercy, but I think that unlikely. I see no other way for you to save those whom you love the most, and stop the killings."

"Mr Christoulides, please explain how you know all this? How do you know what will happen next? And can you tell me why it's happening?" The tone in his voice begged for replies that made sense.

"Why it's happening is easy, Mr Cole. You asked the goddess for help and she gave it to you, willingly. But then you rejected her in favour of a mortal, your wife, your one true love."

"How do you know all this?"

Lukas looked out to sea and then down at Richard, placing a hand on his shoulder. "Like most Fathers, I must know what my children are up to. Sadly, my daughter is up to no good."

"Daughter?" Richard's open-mouth expression and wide staring eyes confirmed his shock.

"Yes, Aphrodite is my daughter."

"Then… that would make you…" He couldn't find the words to speak them.

"Zeus. Yes, Mr Cole, I am."

Richard's Darth Vader moment had come. He stood up, his astonishment and realisation of what he had just heard and long suspected finally revealed in all its glory. "You, are Zeus?" The incredulity of that statement resonated in his mind, like a clanging bell.

"I am."

"But… How is that possible? No. No, no, no. It can't be…" he walked around in a tiny circle, trying hard to get his mind in some sort of order. Now this, would definitely put him in the funny farm if he ever repeated it to anyone else. "Where is the long white robe, the thick white beard, and shoulder length hair? Where are your thunderbolts?"

Lukas smiled, looking at him as if he were more than a friend. "This is the 21st Century, Mr Cole, even gods have to move with the times. I must adopt the modern ways of mortals, just as I did through all the other centuries. I have, so have my brothers, and sisters, and sons and daughters. And by doing this, we have also been able to live among you. But we rarely venture out of our comfort zone, preferring to stay anonymous. We have adapted well to the times, I even have an IPhone." He brandished the gadget in his hand proudly, before returning it to his pocket. "Unfortunately, my daughter is the one who broke tradition, when she decided you were the one she would help. I'm sure you remember your prayer? She answered it and in doing so, bonded herself to you, believing you to be her lover, or, future lover."

"I only asked to come home safely."

"And you did. She kept you safe as promised, but when the time came, you rejected her. She did not expect that and her anger against you has turned to vengeance, which she means to have. Plain and simple, as she sees it, the debt you owe her is one you must pay."

"Can't you stop her? After all, you are her Father, and king of the gods."

"That title has been a little overused, and I don't exactly have dominion over anybody these days, we are more like silent partners, mere witnesses to the ways of mortals. But Aphrodite in her jealousy, for that is what she is, jealous and envious of your life, brought the Scylla out of her lair and into the world. It is ironic that the very creature that comes from a rock and a hard place is now the same that puts you in this position. If I did not know better, I would find that amusing."

"I'm glad you do." The sarcastic comment was lost in the moment, as he sat back down on the beach.

The waves approaching the shore seemed to slow down as if they were listening, eager to capture Zeus' words, whilst seabirds hung in the sky overhead, vanguards to the conversation.

"It's the same question all over again. What do I do now?" He smiled and looked up at Mr Christoulides. "I don't even know what to call you anymore."

"Mr Lukas is fine. Besides, no one would believe such a thing anyway. If you told them. Why would they?"

Lukas was right, he was stuck between a rock and a hard place as no one would believe him, but more than anything else, he had no options left. "As I said, what do I do?"

"Obviously, the authorities have not a clue about what is happening. They suspect something but have no idea what. They will go around in circles as they are looking for evidence and resolutions, but will find none. As we both know, the only person who can do anything is you. Only you, Mr Cole, can kill the Scylla, for reasons which will become apparent when the time comes. Without the creature, Aphrodite will not have the power she thinks she has. Right now, the creature is giving her power as it kills, so it gets stronger and she harnesses that. I have kept her thoughts from you for a while, but my power is waning. I'm sure she will very soon, once again, penetrate your mind, and then own you. Before she does that, you have to find and kill the Scylla. Only you, Richard, can kill it."

"The ancient text says the creature cannot be killed."

"Perhaps that was true in my day, but now the weapons are a lot more powerful than bows and arrows and spears and swords. But that is for you to discover, I cannot help or interfere there."

"Not even a couple of thunderbolts for good measure?" Confused, Richard turned towards the water. "And how the hell do I find her anyway? I don't know where she is." When he turned back he stood on the stones alone. "Finally, now I know how he does that." He brushed the sand off his jeans and pulled the 'wedgie' out.

He stood silently staring at the ocean, the waves growing louder as if they had heard what they needed to, and could resume their perpetual motion without interference. He waited a few more seconds, trying to take in the enormity of what he had learned, before walking back towards Peter's place.

Nicosia

Panayotis had spent several minutes on the phone. He had called all those in-the-know and even those he had not spoken to in a while, for advice and confirmation on what procedure to follow. The search party had collected all the survivors, which numbered thirty; ten bodies were missing, including the captain and the bride. The two youngest were safe with their parents, but Uncle Fabian was lost.

Larnaca's main hospital had taken most of the injured, although three of the more seriously hurt, who were badly burned, needed special treatment, and were taken to Nicosia. Panayotis' next move was to go to the hospital and try to talk to the survivors.

"You were gone a while. Thought I'd have to send out a search party."

"Sorry, got talking."

"With whom?"

"Well…" He was about to say I just met the 'King of the gods' when he stopped and reverted back to a normal explanation. "I bumped into Christoulides. He was in a coffee bar, we chatted, and drank something; he gave me some pointers, on what we should do." He knew the lie wasn't convincing but he had no other alternative.

"What did Mr Christoulides recommend?"

"He said the only way to stop this, is to kill the creature. Definitely kill the Scylla."

"Oh, is that all? Not too bad then! We must just find a mythical beast, which according to its press and PR can't be killed, in a place where we have no idea where it might be… is that about right?"

"Err, yes." The one word answer was all Richard could think to say.

"Piece of piss then."

"When you put it like that, it does seem surreal and far-fetched. But you have only to look at the news to see that maybe it isn't."

Both men sat down again, reflecting on the dilemma before them, then turned towards the television and reached for the remote.

"They think there are ten dead so far, or missing. But they have rescued thirty, crew and passengers." Peter said as he turned the TV back on, and the earlier images repeated, as if on a loop. He flicked buttons, the same story appeared on every Cypriot channel. He settled on RIK 1, just as a mosquito buzzed past his ear. He swatted and missed the offending insect. "Pass me one of those 'mozzie' tabs, will you?"

Richard reached down to the table and picked up a silver strip of tablets designed to keep away mosquitoes and other annoying bugs.

Peter struggled to open the tab. "I can never understand why they only put one tear in these things!"

"I trust we can sort out this Scylla creature a lot better than you and your bloody mosquitoes. And Jesus, how big are these bugs?" Richard smiled, took the tab from him and opened it. "I just hope they are not as big as this other fucker we have to kill."

They laughed together, it was all they could do.

Nicosia hospital was crowded with people, press, the injured, as well as anxious relatives and friends from the boat disaster all huddled together.

Panayotis had a small entourage with him as he pushed open the Emergency Entrance doors and walked through to the back where a young nurse, who seemed a little confused and under pressure, greeted him. She followed the party with her eyes as they grew closer to her desk.

"I am Panayotis Linos, I represent the government." He took from his wallet an official looking ID card and showed it to her.

She nodded her acknowledgement of his identity.

"Please show me to the people from the accident, I need to speak to them."

A police officer, burly in weight and considerably taller than most Cypriot police officers, flanked Panayotis, and as if to add confirmation of his request, also nodded to the nurse, who acknowledged his non-verbal request by pushing the door open and leading Panayotis through.

As Panayotis entered the corridor, there was a made-up triage where several of the patients were either in cubicles, seated on chairs, or laying down on trolleys. The scene was one of confusion, with a good deal of crying mixed with the obvious sounds of pain emanating from behind the curtains. The activity was frenetic, as Doctors, nurses, and auxiliaries made slow progress.

Panayotis stood and watched the activity for a minute. As he scanned the room and corridor, he focused on a young man, who sat on a chair and appeared not badly injured, although he had a large cut over his right eye. The striking thing about the young man was that he wore a dark blue suit, and in the button-hole the fragments of a flower clung to the fabric. He moved slowly over to him.

There was no movement, or acknowledgement of his presence, the eyes remaining squarely glued on the floor, as if searching for an explanation there.

"May I ask you a few questions? My name is Panayotis."

The reaction was the same. The young man continued to stare at the floor, ignoring Panayotis as he tried to repeat his question.

A voice further down the row of seats replied to Panayotis' question. "He can't hear you, has been like that since we got here. Poor sod, got married today. Married and widowed, all in one day."

Panayotis looked down the row of seats to where the voice came from and walked towards it. "Then perhaps you can help me?"

"I can try."

"Who are you?"

"My name is Alan, and I am… was the best man. That's Gary, the groom, the rest are friends and relatives." Alan stood up, revealing legs with bad lacerations and burns, his trousers ripped from the knee down, along with some facial cuts and bruising around his neck and shoulders, but apart from that, he appeared to be managing. "Do you know what happened, what caused the boat to sink?" He asked keenly and pointedly.

"No, not yet, but we have people investigating the accident now. What do you think happened? Can you tell me what you saw, and heard?"

"Maybe, but not here. I think we should go somewhere private, I don't want people to get the wrong idea or start making things up, or get themselves upset."

"I understand," Panayotis took Alan by the arm, guided him down one passage, and into an empty room. He steered the young man inside and closed the door behind them.

As Alan sat down, his legs began to shake a little; the shock of the day was beginning to unfold.

"Would you like some water?" Panayotis handed him a bottle, together with a small plastic cup.

"Better not. They told us not to eat or drink anything until someone saw to us."

"Of course. So, Alan, please take your time and tell me what you saw. What happened out there? And start at the beginning." Panayotis encouraged and sat in the opposite chair.

Alan began to relate the day's events, starting with the civil ceremony in Paphos, the bus ride to the harbour, and the boarding of the *Chastity*.

Panayotis listened for about forty minutes, the words building a picture in his mind. He made small notes in his notepad, that he opened on the Blackberry, listing times, names, and all other pertinent information of the yet to be explained sinking.

Alan stopped a couple of times, especially when it became overwhelming as he relieved the horror, then resumed his tale.

Panayotis recorded not just the events, and usual facts, but also the emotions Alan expressed, and what he said he recalled. One element that came across strongly and often, was the mysterious noise under the vessel, the scraping scratching sound that started the episode, before it sank. He was uncertain what to make of it and thought that possibly, Alan had misheard or became confused amid the commotion and chaos.

But Alan kept repeating that portion of the narrative. "It was that scratching sound under the boat. We all heard it. Something was scraping along the bottom, and it was chilling." He was reliving the terror, his eyes glazed, like a replay, and then he asked. "What do you think it could be?"

Instead of answering, Panayotis continued to write, and thought to himself. *'God, I need to get divers to that spot. Maybe this Mrs Speagal's missing boat is down there, and the Chastity ran into it. But then... what sank her boat?'*

CHAPTER SEVENTEEN

This is no dream

Paphos, evening
After his last meeting with Mr Lukas, Richard needed rest. His brain and body felt drained, but somehow, he had to clear his mind. As he closed his eyes, Lukas' warning words came crashing in. He closed his eyes again, trying hard to digest all that he had discovered.

Lukas had tried to keep her away from him, but his power was fading, even as hers grew stronger. It was simply a matter of time before she had complete control of him. Not just his mind, but his body, and spirit too.

He turned on his side, trying to force himself to fall sleep, and rammed images of his family into his head. Julie, Matthew, and Molly's faces appeared as his mind opened like an old photo album, and he began to turn the pages. His children's life stages materialised; from their first steps, to first words, and through to their schooldays. The special family outings they spent together from their days in the country, enjoying their picnics, to their days at the beach, building sand castles and flying kites, and horseback riding along the shores. Holidays abroad, spent at the pool. He watched them growing up, becoming teenagers, and now young smart adults. And throughout all the pictures and memories, Julie was by his side.

But some pictures, he did not recall, even as the pages turned over and over. For as he reached the last page of the album, another image appeared. It was a stark reminder of his nightmares, showing him the lifeless figure of a young Iraqi boy, lying beside the burnt-out wreck of a car. Slowly, crimson trickled from the child's body, and as it flowed, it began to fill the room, flooding into narrow channels, like tributaries, fanning out across the floor, and into a puddle.

The pool grew around Richard and began to bubble and simmer even as red steam arose from its core. As the blood continued to boil, a form emerged from its centre. First, a face, then, shoulders and a torso, the shape's identity obscured by the sheer amount of blood covering it.

As the figure materialised out of the pool, the face was not instantly recognisable until a drip, drip, drip, began and Richard realised he was staring at himself. The instant he recognised his blood-covered mirror image, it disappeared into the bloody pool, only to resurface into the clearer blue waters of the Mediterranean, where he found himself swimming naked in the ocean. As he looked around, he recognised the place as Petra Tou Romiou.

The warm summer sun stroked his shoulders, but within seconds, it instantly vanished, as he found himself plunged into the dark of night, lit only by the faintest of moonlights. He continued swimming, towards the Rocks, just as he had done the night he chose his true love.

"You remember this," She was back in his head.

He had no power to resist, his mind now a toy for her to play with and use. He swum towards the voice and as he drew closer, he saw her lying across the waves as she had done before.

"This was not supposed to happen. You were to have chosen me. I was your one true love."

He found himself back on the shore.

Ten yards ahead of him stood the goddess pointing out to sea. *"Now, I shall show you what your actions have made me do."*

The night sky flickered, and as lightning flashed wildly across the shoreline and out to sea, the events of recent days, came to life. As he watched, he became a tortured and reluctant spectator, unable to close his eyes or to shut her out.

"Watch, Richard, see what you made me do."

There was not much else to do but obey.

The first scene was of a boy, aged nine, kicking a football. He was on the edge of the shore with not too many people around. A woman in a bikini lay on a beach-chair close-by, her eyes shut, and it looked as if she were asleep. Beside her, placed on a small beach table, was a pair of designer sunglasses, a paperback, and an empty glass.

The boy practiced kicking the ball out to sea and let the waves roll it back. He did this several times before smacking the ball high and long across the breakers. Pitching into the water, he ran through the surf, eager to retrieve his ball. But as he drew deeper into the waves, the beach shelved and he drifted in the current, forcing him further and further away. Ahead of him, the ball bobbed about, and he began to swim towards it, his arms stretching out as he drew closer.

"Go back, leave it." Richard cried out as something began to move below the water and towards the boy, but his warning went unheard.

Before he could react, the entity grabbed and dragged the boy under. Below the waves, he struggled for breath and tried to scream. Suddenly, his body turned dark and Richard saw the first sight of the creature tearing into the child's flesh. As the attack continued, it coloured the water, a deep rich crimson and flavoured it with the sweet scent of blood. The noise of cracking bones and the gush of soft internal organs mixed with seawater created a thick soup of body parts, as blood oozed and flooded, infecting the clarity around him. Thrashing desperately, the boy's last fight was hopeless and empty as the creature's canine heads gouged and gorged on his tender flesh.

Richard tried to avert his eyes, but couldn't, his gaze remaining fixed on the dreadfulness as the creature ravenously devoured its prey.

"This was just the beginning." Her words followed the horror, offering commentary to his visions. *"After this, we had the cliff jumper, and the diver... oh, yes, and the old man, and the policeman."*

Small images of tortured faces flashed before Richard's eyes, like pixels on a computer screen, gruesome, grotesque images of pain and suffering playing out for him, and only him.

"But the best... ah, yes, my sister did us proud with this one. She is so bad, taking away a bride even before she is wet."

The drowning merry-makers amid screams, destruction, and devastation of the wedding boat were the last images broadcasted. By now, his eyes were filled with tears, as he watched the death of boat and passengers evolving before him. Remnants of the disaster floated on the water, debris, human and mechanical, mingled in the bloodied shadows of desolation.

Aphrodite drew closer, and held in her hand three pieces of fabric; a denim square from a pair of men's trunks, another cut from a piece of leather from a diver's wetsuit, and a white square from a wedding dress. *"My sister likes to take souvenirs, but appears to have lost one... Never mind, I am sure it will turn up somewhere."* She folded her hand over and gripped the pieces tightly. *"See what happens when you don't listen? I could go on and on until you agree to be mine, but my sister, as you can see, has the taste for it now, so really, it is up to you. But next time, know who it will be?"*

Richard snapped his eyes open. He was standing on a shoreline, the same one where he had last spoken to Mr Christoulides. This was no dream, and how he was transported there only she knew.

Peter was on the phone when he walked back into the room.

He nodded and looked at his watch, almost eight o'clock.

"Yes, Sheila, I hope that is not too inconvenient for you. Yes, I do appreciate it, thank you…" His words were almost conciliatory as he smiled a sarcastic smile, knowing she couldn't see it. "I'll come over early tomorrow. Yes, thank you… No, I won't disturb you if you just leave the garage door open. I can find what I need, thanks. Bye." He put the phone down. "Bitch." The simple word left nothing to the imagination. "Hey, pal, where have you been? I checked on you a couple of hours ago, looked again about half an hour ago and you were gone. What's up?"

"I had a nasty dream and needed to get some air." The explanation was tame at best but it would have to do.

"Had any more bright ideas how we find this Scylla creature and your goddess?" Peter asked while pointing to the piles of pictures occupying the coffee table.

Richard wanted to confess, badly, especially now that he was being targeted by the Mistress of the Rock. He desperately wanted to tell someone, but knew he dare not. Not even Peter. "No." The glum response was about all he could muster with his head still in a spin.

"Well, then, I have an idea." Peter was almost bursting with excitement, as if he had solved The Times Crossword, and sat down beside Richard. "One of my friends runs a business network. You might even have heard of them, they have them in the UK, where people meet to exchange sales leads and try to drum up business. All kinds of people go to these meetings and I met someone a couple of months back at the local one in Paphos. A German woman, Rycinne Haller. Really nice lady, about our age, or maybe slightly older.

"She said that if I ever wanted to try hypnosis to cure a problem, like a phobia, or cut out smoking, to call her. I told her I didn't smoke anymore… Anyway, she gave me her card and on it says she specialises in regression. It could be a long shot, but she might also help find the creature, if she can go back through your dreams. Perhaps there's something in them that you have subconsciously put to the back of your mind. What do you say, give it a go?"

"I guess it could work, as we don't have much else to go on. But I am a bit sceptical of these kinds of treatments."

"You, sceptical? Don't make me laugh. After all you've asked me to believe in, that is almost comical. Well, almost."

His wry smile made Richard feel a little easier.

Peter took the phone in his hand and began to dial the number on the card.

'Peter has a point,' Richard thought. *'And if I can see things others can't then why should I be dubious about this proposal?'*

"Okay," Peter said a few minutes later. "We are set for tomorrow. We'll go meet Rycinne, and see what she can do for you. But first, I will go pay a visit to the old house. Won't be too long, I only have to pick something up."

"I heard you talking to Sheila. Have you told her I'm here?"

"Not bloody likely, she is just about speaking to me. If she knew you were here she would totally ignore me."

"Why, what did I do to her?"

"It's a long story and not worth telling now. Maybe one day…"

"What are you picking up?"

"Some tools I need, for a job I am looking to do. I suggest we get an early night. But now, a night-cap, and then bed." Peter moved over to the cabinet which housed the few drinks he had stowed away.

"Seems like a plan."

Two Remy Martins were poured carefully into the crystal brandy glasses.

"Cheers." The two glasses chinked.

As soon as Richard reached his bedroom and undressed, the brandy did its trick. He passed peacefully into sleep, no last-minute images of the goddess, or the terrors she would try to evoke. Just a cool peaceful darkness as he closed his eyes.

Zeus was doing his best to keep her away.

CHAPTER EIGHTEEN

Explanations

Nicosia, Sunday Night

Panayotis had returned to his office in Nicosia hours previously but was still up. He had consumed almost half a dozen cups of coffee, Greek and instant, to keep himself alert and focused. He had gone over Alan's statement and those of the others. He had no answers for the disaster, just a lot of questions. And the suppositions he had before him, like most of this disturbing case, didn't make sense either.

Reports of a large black shadow circling under the boat seemed too bizarre for serious deliberation but it was a recurring theme among the witnesses, so he needed to at least give it some thought. He also had Jenny Speagal's testimony, whose story of the two big red eyes had a smidgen of merit when added to the other findings. But he still needed a logical reason for the disaster.

For a second, he considered the idea of the lost diving boat under the water, but dismissed it, sure other passing craft would have reported something on their radars. A submarine? Too contrived. And there were no whales to speak of in these waters. He was even starting to come around to the idea of the Ayia Napa Sea Monster, but that was pure fantasy. For him, there had to be a rational explanation.

He called for the *Chastity's* mechanical log, to check on its maintenance; it was being rushed by motorcycle courier from Paphos. From the local reports, he had received from the harbour area and around the fort, most restaurants were quiet. No one felt much like dining out on such a solemn and sad evening.

Panayotis reclined into the large leather chair, lifted his feet up onto the desk to try relaxing, and shut his eyes. The day had been long and difficult and what started with a memorial service was ending the same way. He opened his eyes, leaned forward, and grabbed the last report off the pile; it was a short statement on Lenny Speagal's disappearance. "Maybe this is it." He mused.

The missing boat was said to be somewhere near the location where the *Chastity* went down, it might have stayed submerged for a while and then bobbed up. If it had a mast or rigging, that could have lodged itself to the *Chastity's* hull, dragged it along, and produced those scratching noises no one seemed to forget. And didn't people say the simplest answer was often overlooked? Besides, he had nothing else right now. He reached into his jacket pocket, and pulled out the notes from Mrs Speagal. All this nonsense about red eyed monsters... He took his phone and called the number. It rang twice then went to answerphone.

"Hello, *and thank you for calling Sun Divers. The operation is temporarily closed, but we hope to be back soon. Thank you again for calling. Oh, and if this is you, Lenny Speagal, get your arse back here fast. Bye for now.*"

He was about to leave a message then decided against it, Jenny was not around. But he had her notes and an idea where her wreck could be. He needed it checked, and quick.

Myron Edwards

Monday morning

Panayotis awoke to a numbing pain in his leg. Cramp had set in and he bounced around the office trying desperately to regain normality to his blood stream. He cavorted and twirled his body, rubbing his leg vigorously with one hand; short pins and needle pains penetrated through the cramp and he began to regain composure as his impromptu office dance ended abruptly. Wiping his eyes, he looked down at his jotted notes, which he had transferred into a small writing pad from his Blackberry.

He moved across the room to his small office toilet and ran the hot and cold water into the sink. He took out his toothbrush and toothpaste, essentials he kept for such emergencies, and began his morning routine. After he washed and cleaned his teeth, he checked his cabinet and found the one spare white shirt he knew he had and put it on. He decided to leave his tie off, preferring the open neck, rather than the austere 'suited and booted' look.

The phone messages on his office mobile numbered six. As he opened it, he saw that five of them were from Christina. The other was from the President's office.

Only one newspaper linked the sinking of the *Chastity* to the young Romanian boy and the British tourist. That paper was Phileleftheros, the Greek language newspaper. Journalist Tassos Evrapidou had detailed some of the chronology and events and tried to piece them together as some sort of serial occurrence. The premise of the story was well thought out and made for an interesting read, which Panayotis quickly dismissed as sensationalism as he went through the paper in front of him.

Christina had collated all information from Paphos, together with some of the medical reports from Nicosia and Larnaca, delivered them to Panayotis, and together, they sat going over and over the statements and documents, as well as the medical references.

It was only 8am and already Panayotis was yawning. He was still waiting for news about the other boat but nothing had been found so far. They would have to keep searching. Only one thing was certain, there were now two boats sunk.

Paphos

Peter got up early. Richard's meeting wasn't until 9:30am so if he went quickly, he could do Pissouri in an hour there and back, or maybe a bit less, if Sheila did not accost him. He downed his coffee swiftly, picked up his car keys, and closed the door quietly behind him.

He cut through the early morning traffic and speed-traps, accelerating and decreasing speed when he thought a police car was nearby. He knew the routine fairly well, where they positioned themselves, and he was quite adept at dodging and diving in and out of the traffic lanes. He was becoming more Cypriot than Brit with each passing year he was on the island.

Instead of taking the highway, he took the old road, as it would take him past Geroskipou, which was a small quaint village complete with Orthodox Church and village square. It was also the site of one of the lesser known Cypriot industries, where they produced what the English call Turkish Delight and the Cypriots, Greek Delight, for obvious reasons. The sweets were a particular favourite of Peter's. They came in different flavours and hexagon-shaped boxes, with the confectionery always coated in a white sugary powder, which he always got covered in when he dipped into them.

But today, he was not stopping to buy any, although, he noticed as he glanced at his watch, a couple of tourist coaches had stopped and people were beginning to pile out across the square and into the local cafes as he drove past them.

Peter pushed on through the village and out onto the country road for a couple more kilometres before he passed the Elea Golf Resort, his local course, and sped down the road en-route to Pissouri. He passed several references to Aphrodite's temple and a large poster which said Petra Tou Romiou, Aphrodite's Rock. Beneath the letters, was a batch of graffiti, in various languages. Most said, from what Peter could make out, "*No*, or, ***nothing there***, or, ***what Rock***?" followed by a crude drawing of the bare-breasted goddess. He accelerated past the sign, turning left to the motorway.

Richard slept sounder and longer than he had managed in ages then showered and dressed quickly. He was feeling somewhat apprehensive as he sipped some cold water to refresh himself; the last days of his trip were fast approaching and whatever his fate was would soon be decided, and apparently, not by him.

Peter had left breakfast on the table; cereals, orange juice, and a croissant. The pot of tea was cold, so Richard opted for a coffee instead. As he sat eating his fare, he stared at a pile of pictures and the notes lying on top of the table. Reaching forward, he prised one of the images from the heap. As he looked at it, he confirmed Peter's earlier statement that she was, "an ugly Mother" then added, "And guess what, I am going to kill you."

Arriving at his old house, Peter realised it was a while since he'd been there. On the outside, not much had changed. The patio had recently been cleaned and the windows washed, but some of the plants Sheila kept in their pots in front had been replaced, as he didn't recognise them from his previous visit. Strange, how he never took notice of what plants and shrubs grew in the garden or the patio before, but now he did. Perhaps it was Sheila's subtle way of showing him she had moved on.

Opening the garage door, he moved inside, trying to keep the noise to a minimum, and found what he was looking for; a long metal box about four-feet in length with two heavy padlocks keeping it secure. He opened the locks with the key he kept on his keychain, took out a gravy coloured canvas bag, closed the lid behind him, and made his way back to the car. Placing the bag inside, he closed the boot, gently. As he started the car, he took one last look at his old house. He was not sure but thought he saw one of the net curtains move as he reversed out of the driveway and into the road.

Richard sat waiting impatiently, alternating his pacing from patio to kitchen, and between those movements, he switched the television on and off. The Greek channels carried mostly soaps; one he watched for a few seconds, seemed to be Mexican, dubbed into Greek. He thought it was Mexican as the main hero appeared wearing a large yellow sombrero in most of his scenes, and sported a Zapata style moustache, which obscured his bottom lip completely when he spoke in whatever language he was using.

He poured and drank another coffee; he would also need the loo before going to meet the hypnotist. The idea spooked him. He was reticent about meeting her, but knew he should. He had to discover where the goddess would be, although, he imagined Peter was looking at this as a bit of an adventure and humouring him.

And why shouldn't he? No one else had thus far seen the goddess or had any of the disturbing visions. Peter was being asked to believe his word only, and that, in the scheme of things, was a tall order for anyone to go along with. It just went to show how good a mate he really was.

Peter opted to save time and headed down the highway. Driving faster than he should, he glanced at his watch; just 8:30, plenty of time to get back, pick up Richard, and get to Rycinne's before 9:30. He checked his rear-view mirror for approaching police cars. Seeing an empty road, he pushed his foot down onto the accelerator and pulled away, the speedometer reading 120 as the car moved into overdrive.

He rounded the top bend at Petra Tou Romiou and at the brow of the hill looked down to the empty beach, where the rocks had once stood. A small group had already assembled from what he could see, as he sped away from the site.

Ahead in the distance, he saw someone standing by the roadside but couldn't make out what gender the person might be. A guy broken down or a female in distresses? He slowed down. Approaching the figure, his eyes fixed on those of a woman. She was alone and he slowed down more, the gears changing automatically.

As he drew closer, he saw her quite clearly. She was young, in her late twenties, possibly early thirties, with light brown hair and a gypsy-type multi-patterned skirt. Her top was white, almost pristine, and she had open sandals on her feet.

Feeling somewhat chivalrous and seeing no other vehicles in sight, Peter decided he would stop and slowed down the car. As he turned to look in the rear-view mirror to check the road behind, a female voice called out his name beside him.

"Peter."

He almost crashed the car.

He turned to where the voice had come from and afterwards back to look for the girl at the roadside, but she was no longer there. He pushed his foot down on the pedal again, the only thought in his head, 'I need a drink.'

CHAPTER NINETEEN

Consultation and Candles

Peter's car pulled up outside just after nine. He got out, walked around the back, and opened the boot, took out the canvas bag and went inside.

Richard merely glanced in his direction as he sat on the patio finishing the last dregs of his coffee.

With the bag in hand, Peter plonked himself down in the chair next to him. "Any more coffee? Preferably black, and strong." He breathed in, leaned across the table, and pushed his cup towards Richard.

Richard lifted the lid to discover that enough might be left over and poured it into the offered cup. "You okay?" He asked, sensing that something wasn't right.

"Bloody Sheila always gets under my skin. The bitch wants more." Peter's quick excuse for his demeanour gave certain credence to his posture.

Richard didn't press his friend any further. Leave well alone was probably the best action right now.

As Peter picked up his coffee and drank the tepid liquid, it dawned on him that he was now the one keeping secrets. "When you're ready, we can go."

"What's in the bag?" Richard queried.

"I'll show you when we get back." Peter grabbed his car keys, took the bag inside before locking the house, and turned the alarm on.

Which was an odd move for Richard, because he had never seen him set the alarm before. But he decided against a barrage of questions, even if something was amiss.

Because at the moment, he had more urgent worries of his own to think about.

The two got in the car, and pulled away, narrowly missing the motorbike that was about to overtake them.

Panayotis had recovered from his night's sleep. He had read not once but twice the documents before him, and called the President's office. The conversation was fairly succinct and Panayotis knew he had to act quickly to stem any speculation from press and media about what had happened to the *Chastity*, but all logic told him that none of what he had read so far made any sense. Well, none that he could justify as an explanation.

He turned on his laptop, waited for the screen to parade its collection of icons, and when fully functional, he Googled the word Cryptid. Dozens and dozens of pages emerged, some with images. On one of the lines, he found a reference to the Ayia Napa Sea Monster, and clicked the page. Was it possible this was the answer for the Speagels' boat vanishing? Yes or no, he still had to try something! But a sea monster in Ayia Napa… that was stretching things just a little too far.

Peter pulled into the McDonalds and parked just at the rear of the car park.

"We're going to meet her here?"

"No, her place is just a block down. But parking's a real bugger around there, so I use this place from time to time and nearly always go get a Big Mac afterwards."

"Okay, lead on then, and let's see what your friend has to say."

Both climbed out of the car with trepidation about what was to follow.

After locking the car, they made their way out of the parking lot and down the road, turning a sharp left before going behind some delivery vans parked across the front of the 'So Easy' shop.

"It's just up those steps, second floor. Her name is on the door. After you."

Leading the way, Richard climbed the steps two at a time, reached the second floor not quite out of breath, and rang the brass door bell.

The door buzzed and opened automatically. Inside, the hallway was bland, painted in an all familiar shade of magnolia that needed a fresh coat soon. Only two pictures hung on the wall, one was of Paris, and the other of the Pyramids of Giza. Obviously, places visited and displayed to confirm that status.

Peter knocked on the inside door.

That too swung open, but this time, someone was behind it.

"Hello, Rycinne." Peter greeted the woman with a kiss on both cheeks.

Richard stood behind him, waiting his cue.

"This is Richard, whom I told you about."

"Hello, Richard, it's good to meet the man who changed this island."

"Oh, I didn't realise you knew who I was." He was a shade surprised by the woman's comment then smiled awkwardly at his notoriety and waited for her to say something else.

As he studied her, he noticed a thin scar under her chin; one that he had already seen, or at least, was pretty similar to one he had seen before. That scar belonged to a young woman named Amanda, who had throat cancer, a good friend of Julie's. Perhaps Rycinne had cancer at one point too, but unlike Amanda, had recovered.

Rycinne took a seat and motioned for the men to do the same. She didn't say anything straight away, merely observed, her eyes scanning Richard's face, looking at every crack and crevice, especially his rapidly deepening furrowed brow and fast receding hairline. She stared for a few more seconds, this time looking deep into his eyes, which appeared heavy and tired and just a little red from lack of sleep.

He did his best not to stare back, but it was difficult, as he too scanned her face. She was unquestionably older than both of them, probably more sixty than fifty, but her figure was remarkably trim, and she looked very agile, which, she proved when she got up from her chair, scampered across the room, and returned with an electronic notepad.

She switched the device on and linked it to a PC on her desk. This was attached to some sort of audio device which began to emit barely audible high frequencies. "Oh, sorry, I didn't realise it was still switched on."

As he sat listening, he heard her accent clearly for the first time, and there was no hint of German. Her voice could best be described as cosmopolitan, with no specific inflection, just a tone that undulated up and down, first in a soft lilt and then into a more guttural pronunciation, especially when she spoke words like "under and control" which she did often, to explain her technique.

Peter watched in silence as Rycinne explained the methods she used for treating her clients.

She called them clients, not patients, because, as she said, she never treated anyone as if they were sick, simply clients who required her services.

Richard adjusted his position on the chair and listened.

"First, Richard… do you mind me calling you by your first name?"

"No, it's fine."

"I use a mix of old and new. I don't go for all those flashing lights, bells, and whistles that some people do, I prefer a more old-fashioned approach for establishing rapport. I will ask you to do only two things for me, the first is to close your eyes, and the second, to take all your clothes off."

Both men's eyes and mouths opened wide in shock.

Rycinne laughed loudly, "No, I am joking. Sorry, but you should have seen your faces."

Peter's face was equally red, having thought the strange request was for real.

"Alright now, let's be serious for a few minutes." Rycinne stretched over the table and took out three scented candles from a drawer. She placed each one in turn into a holder, then reached for a box of matches, and struck one to light the candles. She got up, walked to the window, and pulled down the shutters. The bijou potted-plant interior taking on an eerie glow as the flames flickered and their faces caught the reflection of the dancing lights.

A stillness entered the room, but it wasn't eerie, more mystical.

Rycinne moved across to Richard, switched on her PC, and an audio track began to play a soft, scarcely audible chant.

Peter sat back into the shadows as the atmosphere in the room became almost intimate.

"Now, all I want you to do is relax. I want you to stare at the candles, nothing else, just keep looking at them. You will notice they are different sizes, the larger one has a bigger flame, the middle one less, and the smaller one little or no flame, just keep watching the small one. In a few seconds, the flame will go out. When it does, I want you to close your eyes and keep them closed. There is no need for you to say anything, just nod."

Richard did so, and it was as she said, for within a few seconds, the small candle went out. He followed his cue to close his eyes, all light gone from his vision.

"I am going to take you back; back, back, back, back through your lifetime. I want you to imagine there is a road ahead of you. Do you see it? It is your life's road. As you can see, there are many signposts on this path, early days, army days, married days, family days, present day, or days past, *which* one do you want to take?"

"I think I need to go down days past. I know the other roads well… I will go down days past."

"Alright. Good. Now walk slowly and tell me what you see."

"I see a highway. It is full of dead people, women, children, soldiers… there are Arabic signs and vehicles covered in holes and all around me there are fires burning and the smell of charred flesh. I see soldiers, dressed in uniform going through the wrecks, shooting at some of the bodies, making sure they are dead. Now, I see a shadowy figure… a woman coming from behind one of the burnt-out cars, she is all in black. I can't see her face, but she is walking towards me, pointing at me, thinks I'm to blame for this. *'No, it's not me, it's not my fault,'* I scream back at her but she just keeps coming with her pointing finger. But it's not made of flesh, it's bone, her fingers are just bones, like her hand, and her face. Oh, God, her face… it's hideous, she has no eyes, just a mass of loose flapping skin covering her head, and from that skin, maggots are crawling, burrowing, emptying out from the holes. They scatter across the ground, crawling all around me, and still she walks towards me. I can't get away. I am trying to run…"

Peter reached over to Rycinne, urging her to stop, but she resisted the movement.

"Has she gone, are you still on that road, Richard?"

"My legs feel heavy, but yes, she is moving away from me. I am getting away from her."

"Has she gone, Richard?"

"Yes, she's gone, the road is empty. Up ahead, I see trees and there are flowers growing close by. I can't see what they are, but they are brightly coloured, red and yellow ones, and a mix of purple and pink. There are small animals running around too, rabbits and a fawn and there are birds on the branches and I can hear them singing. The forest is very green and the sun is splitting the trees with its bright beams and I can hear water running from a stream nearby. I can hear the forest, it's talking to me."

"Do you recognise the place?"

"No, I have never been here before. But it does feel familiar and I don't know why."

"Can you see anything, or anyone else?"

"There is another road to the left, a narrow one, like a beach road, it leads downwards."

"Do you want to go down that road, Richard?"

"Yes, I am going down now. Ah, it's a beach road, leading to the sea. I can hear the ocean, the waves are crashing loudly against the shore, like a roar, but as I get closer the sound stops. I can't hear them anymore, there is just silence, and stillness, even the air seems static, nothing or nobody is moving. I can see the sun on the horizon, it is setting. The sea and the sky are folding together, the blend of colours magical, like a regal turquoise. Ahead of me, the shore is empty. No, wait… there is something there, stirring in the water but I can't see it clearly. Now, somebody else is there. I can see her, she is by the water's edge."

"Who is it, Richard?"

"I can tell it's a woman. Yes, a woman, she is calling me. Like the other one before, she is also holding out her hand, telling me to come forward. I can feel my legs moving even though I don't want them to, but they are going towards her. The sea behind her is starting to become very choppy as if something is below the waves, waiting to emerge. The woman keeps calling me forward, I don't want to go, but I can't stop myself. The sea throws up a deluge of water and out of the spray comes a creature not of this world… I can't look at it, I can't, but I am forced to. I must run away from here but my legs are dragging me forward, I am losing my footing. I have to run, run away, help me to run away."

"Run, Richard, you can run. Just turn and run away from there." Rycinne took one of his hands and squeezed it gently.

Peter again moved to stop the session, but Rycinne's eyes flashed at him that he must let her continue.

"I am running. My heart is racing, I can feel it… pumping, pumping, and I am still running. I can see the road, the one to the forest. I am going up that road now, looking behind me but no one is there. I can stop now, I can stop. I must stop."

"Yes, Richard, stop now. Take it easy, find a place to relax. Can you see somewhere?"

"There is a small old tree stump in front of me, I can sit there. It's gone quiet now, the forest noises have all stopped. Something is happening, the wind is rushing through the leaves and trees. The sun is losing its shine, the shadows are growing longer, and I can hear something in the ground, like a thumping noise across the earth, a rasping, raking sound that scuttles the bushes in front of it, bending them over, cracking the twigs… I can't see what it is but it is getting closer. The noise is really loud now, like a pounding on the earth, I can feel the air close to me is hot, I can…"

"What is it, Richard?" Rycinne grabbed his hand and squeezed it tighter. "Tell me." The panic in her voice was becoming obvious as she wrestled with Richard's subconscious.

"I can feel pain, in my leg, and there is blood flowing. A deep wound has opened and the flesh is gaping. I can't stop the blood. The pain and the agony, I can't…"

"Richard, listen to me when I tell you, I want you to open your eyes and look straight at the large candle and blow out the flame. Do you hear me, Richard? Blow out the flame of the large candle."

"I can't open my eyes… I can only feel the pain… I can't… σκότος."

"Now, Richard, open your eyes, open them." Rycinne's voice had risen an extra decibel as she yelled at him.

He opened his eyes, looked straight at the large candle, and blew it out.

Rycinne stretched across and took his hand. Then seeing his face covered in sweat, she removed a tissue from the box on the table, and wiped away his perspiration.

Peter reached over to the water dispenser and pushed a plastic cup under to draw out some ice-cold liquid, which he handed to Richard.

He swallowed it down without even tasting it.

Rycinne blew out the last flame. All three sat back. With the session over, the questions, and hopefully answers began.

She took hold of Richard's hand to comfort him again. "Are you alright?"

"Fine, fine." He repeated the word to reassure her.

"That was quite a session. I have many questions as no doubt you have. Do you remember what you saw?"

"Yes." He pushed the empty plastic cup under the water machine and drew another cup, this time drinking it slower.

"I have never seen such a vivid PTSD demonstration. Usually, the client in these circumstances finds the repressed memory in, shall we say, pieces, fragments of recollections, not as a coherent story, more like a jigsaw, where the images become the pieces and are placed in their various slots filling up the spaces. But in your case, you have a living narrative. Your memory and your dreams, if that is what they are, combine, so that the story moves from one scene to the next seamlessly. It is quite extraordinary. Your experiences in the Gulf War are the catalyst, but beyond them there is something else buried much deeper, something that wants to penetrate your consciousness, but can't. I know this sounds very Freudian, but it is just my interpretation."

"Do you have any idea who the woman is?" Richard asked, as he too was becoming fascinated by Rycinne's explanation and wanted to learn more.

"Which one, the one by the sea or the woman in black?"

"The one in black."

"The woman in black is, I believe, a metaphor for death. She haunts you, follows you in your dreams, perhaps because she thinks you have cheated her. Maybe you should have been killed on Highway 80. Yes, I know all about it, Peter gave me some background on your problems. But it has not affected my deliberations. If anything, it has clarified my explanation a little further. The PTSD you suffer is the reason behind your dreams and your memory. I believe it manifests itself in your unconscious world then penetrates your reality. Which sometimes explains why it is difficult for you to separate them. This is why, in my opinion, your dreams are so vivid, because you can't tell what is real and what isn't. Does that make sense?"

"Yes, in a roundabout way it does. Is there anything I can do?" He finished his water and placed the plastic cup on the table.

"This is difficult for me to say, Richard, but to treat this, you need to seek professional help, some psychiatrist or specialist who perhaps can clean your memories."

"I see. This is something Peter and I discussed earlier and I am resigned to do."

"I do have one other question." Rycinne moved forward on her chair. "When you were in the forest the second time, you spoke one Greek word, or, it sounded Greek. Do you know what you said?"

"No, sorry, I don't remember that."

"Let me play it to you. I record all of my sessions, so I can go back over them later." Rycinne pressed the button on the device. "I think it was about here."

The recorder began to play the last section of the recording.

"Richard, listen to me when I tell you, I want you to open your eyes and look straight at the large candle and blow out the flame. Do you hear me, Richard? Blow out the flame of the large candle."

"I can't open my eyes... I can only feel the pain... I can't.... σκότος."

"What is that word? Where did you hear it before, and why did you say it?"

"I don't know, sorry. I don't recall saying it."

"No matter, I will find out. I am sure it's Greek but maybe some dialect that I am not familiar with. I only know one phrase in Greek. 'Then milou Eligniga boli kalla.' Which means, I do not speak Greek very well."

"Well, I don't speak it all." Richard smiled back and took Rycinne's hand. "How much do I owe you?"

"Call it twenty-five Euros. I normally charge forty but this has been fascinating. With your permission, I would like to add this session to my list of clients' portfolios. I am collating, and your session is just remarkable."

"No problem, please feel free. Thank you once again, and I will take your advice about finding someone to help me."

"I would really like to get to know you better, Richard. There is something inside you that is so deeply hidden I can't prise out of you, especially not at the first session, but I would like to try. Could we arrange for another session next week? We can have coffee and then do it after, how does that appeal to you?"

"I would like that, if you think it can help."

"I am sure it can, but in the meantime, I need to do some more research."

The two men stood up, both kissed Rycinne on the cheeks, and said their goodbyes. As Richard followed Peter down the stairs this time, both were anxious to speak, but didn't. They walked back to the car in silence, got in, and waited for the moment.

"I know where she is, or rather, where she will be. And I know what time she will be there."

"You didn't say anything in there." Peter pointed out.

"It wasn't necessary, but I know now where and how to find them."

Peter started the car.

"Aren't you going to have your Big Mac?"

"Not today. I think we'd better get back to the house, we have things to discuss." Peter revved the engine, his foot pressing down harder on the pedal before releasing it and letting the car drive off through the car park.

CHAPTER TWENTY

Paperwork and Politics

Cyprus likes committees; it is a major part of their operations and organisations. Whether it's political, cultural, industrial, or financial, each and every one has to have a committee. And the recent events of the past few days offered the perfect opportunity to form another one. This one consisted of delegates and heads of government, tourist organisations, and business as well as the local municipalities. The machinations of these committees were to offer cohesion, co-operation, and where applicable, compromise, which meant only one thing, delegation, and that was always the most difficult part. Because with delegation comes responsibility and no one wanted to take it on, especially for the present tragic events. However, the wheels were already turning, albeit slowly, but nevertheless in motion.

The President had already met with the British Ambassador and both had offered full support in their own way. The British, by providing resources from their military bases on the island and the President, affording full cooperation in any inquiry. The authorities had begun delving deeper into what had caused the *Chastity* disaster and small flotillas of boats from the police, army, and the coastguard had taken up positions at the site.

On-board forensic experts had flown from Greece and the UK to discover the cause, working along with their Cypriot counterparts. In a funny kind of way, they had formed a committee of their own, as they went about the business of discovery.

Panayotis found himself in a committee; in fact, this one was a sub-committee, which was also looking at the *Chastity*, something which he had some knowledge of but not enough to make any clear judgement on how and what might have occurred. It was true the wheels on this particular juggernaut were moving, but oh, so slowly.

Mr. Christoulides' assumption that the authorities would be going around in circles was quite correct and justified that any resolution or decision on their part would be a long time coming, if ever. Besides, they had to have more meetings and that meant only one thing, more committees.

London, Angel Islington, Chrissy's flat
For Chrissy, the situation was black and white, as in front of her, on her desk, were a set of papers with cut-out articles all relating to Barry's death. Black bold letters filled the white spaces where Barry's name, gender, and age had already been inserted. The space underneath, cause of death, was just a short one line handwritten sentence, *pending coroner's judgement*. She picked up the newspaper which lay on the table next to the opened envelopes. It was a day old.

She had highlighted the second column with her blue biro pen. *"Wedding Boat sinks off Cyprus coast."* About three-quarters of the way, down the two columns, one sentence was also highlighted. *Police believe this has no connection to the disappearance of British tourist Barry Rochester, who drowned in Cypriot waters, just over a week ago.* Already, Barry's death was old news.

London, Earls Court
Greg too, had a set of forms on his table in front of him. These were applications from the Australian High Commission, titled Emigration to Australia. He picked one

of the pages and began to read. He had made his mind up, he was going, and he was going alone.

Larnaca Hospital

For Elena Petrakis, this past month had been the worst of her short life; she had lost a potential lover, and her workload had almost brought her to the brink of chucking it all in. But unfortunately for Elena, her Hippocratic Oath meant there was no such luxury. She was carrying this burden on her own, with little support to help her.

In the past twenty-four hours, she had done most of the autopsies from the boat herself. Larnaca hospital had invited her over to help them and she agreed. The paperwork piled in stacks; each of the deceased tagged and given a number.

All British bodies from the disaster were to be repatriated, an agreement made by the President and the British Ambassador. If needed, military aircraft would fly the bodies to the UK, but both Cypriots and British were looking to avoid it.

The one thing no one wanted was turning this tragedy into some sort of political exercise. A military escort might do that, so they were working with the undertakers on the island to facilitate enough commercial aircraft to do the job. But until that was completed, the bodies would stay at the morgue.

Elena completed another piece of paperwork and filed it away, as she pushed another body back into cold storage. The Cypriot bodies would be buried within the next day or so, but the bodies of two Czech stewardesses and one Bulgarian waiter had also been placed in cold storage, pending the decision on what to do with them.

They got back from Rycinne's within twenty minutes of leaving the car park. Peter stopped and almost ran up the small stairs onto the patio, furtively looking over his shoulder as he punched in the code to allow them entry.

Richard followed him, watching with some interest as he switched off the alarm.

Peter went straight to the lounge and pulled the shutters down tight. Closed, they made the room turn dark even though it was still daylight outside. Next, he turned all the lights on.

'God, he looks crazy,' Richard thought and continued to watch him.

Peter looked behind the curtains and under the sofa, as if something, or someone, might be hiding in the room.

"Hey, slow down, what is the matter?" Richard grabbed Peter by one shoulder to calm him down, his concern genuine. "What the hell is the matter, you are jumpy. What is it?"

Anxious and nervy looks were all over Peter's face as he dropped onto the sofa. He looked at Richard, and could almost feel the sweat running down the back of his neck even if he couldn't see it. "I have to tell you something. Up until today, I thought all this, you and the goddess, and the Scylla, was a crock of shit, but was willing to go along with it for your sake. I thought, just play along, get the man some help when you can, and see him through it, God knows he's had a rough time. I wanted to believe you, and your story, especially when you told me Julie had also been a witness. But somehow, I couldn't as much as I tried, especially after yesterday."

"Yesterday?" Richard probed.

"Remember when you went out for your walk? I followed you from a distance. You were on the beach on your own, talking to yourself."

"When I met Lukas?"

"Yes, then. Only I couldn't see him and I doubt anyone else could either, because he wasn't there. Even after that, I thought, it's okay, play along, just humour the old bastard."

"Thanks." Richard's face began to glow red with pent-up subdued anger and frustration for his friend.

"No, really, I just went along with it. Besides, I wanted to help you."

"So, then why are you telling me this now? What has happened since yesterday?" Richard's anger tempered as he posed the questions.

"Rich, I honestly wanted to believe you, but all logic told me it was your imagination, your PTSD acting overtime. I just went along with it, but today… after today, I believe you."

"Because of what Rycinne said?"

"No, nothing to do with her, and that's the strange part, although, she did put some meat onto the story. I believe you because of what I saw and heard today."

"What did you see while you were out alone?"

"How do you know it was then?"

"You were as tense as you are now, and told me nothing was wrong. So, what happened?"

"I think I saw your goddess."

Richard stood up and sat down again. He didn't know what reaction to give to Peter's statement. "What do you mean you think you saw the goddess?"

"I was driving back from Sheila's and at the top of the hill at Petra Tou Romiou I saw a few people on the beach. Usual tourists, with cameras snapping shots of where the rocks used to be, so I drove on. About a hundred yards on there was a figure at the roadside. Naturally, I assumed it was someone with a broken-down car. As I got closer, I realised it was a woman, dressed in a sort of multi-coloured gypsy skirt and her top was white, shimmering in the early sunlight. Somewhere in her twenties, or thirties, with light brown hair that appeared curly and she was beautiful. I slowed down, turned to look in the driver's mirror to see what was behind me, and a woman's voice spoke my name beside me. Fuck,

Richard, I almost crashed the car. I swerved, holding the wheel tight, and thank God no one was behind me. When I looked back, she was gone… there was nothing, nobody there. I know I didn't imagine it, and I know what I saw and heard was real. So, yes, in the words of Davy Jones "I'm a believer." I apologise it has taken me so long to grasp and accept." Peter looked straight at Richard.

Their bond had suddenly become stronger and unbreakable.

"And I never wanted to get you mixed up in this. Well, not like you are now, and it should be me apologising. I too wanted to believe it was all just in my mind again, but now you know it isn't." Richard leaned back on the sofa, thoughts running through his head, and most of them related to what he had to do next.

Before he had time to assess further, Peter leaned forward and supplied the answer.

"This is what I picked up at Sheila's today." He stooped down to open the bag, took out a 12-gauge shotgun and a small 45-calibre Springfield service pistol, and handed them over.

"Where did you get these?" Richard asked with astonishment, a shocked expression on his face.

"Long story. Well, not so long, but let's have a drink, and I'll tell you."

CHAPTER TWENTY-ONE

Loose Ends

Oroklini, early evening

Jenny Speagel had not spoken to Mr Linos since leaving the police station. She sat at her kitchen table. In front of her were two piles; one, a batch of unopened envelopes, and in the other, a batch of photographs, mostly of Lenny in his various guises.

Picking up the envelopes, she walked across to the rubbish bin, dumped them into it then returned to the table, and began to sift through the pictures. She checked the kitchen clock on the wall; just after seven. The taxi would be here in another ten minutes. The suitcase beside her was already labelled and the small carrier bag next to it needed just one thing, the small box she had now filled with Lenny's pictures. She had decided to get away, whatever had taken the boat and Lenny may also have its sights on her.

She finished her cigarette and stubbed it out in the ashtray. She rarely smoked but under the circumstances it just felt like the right thing to do, though she was not sure why. She left a big note on the table, just in case she was wrong.

"Gone to Mum's." Jen X

Peter re-entered the room, two large ice-cold Keo bottles in hand. "I think we can forget glasses, don't you?" He chinked his bottle against Richard's and both took a long deep swig.

"You were going to tell me about these?" Richard picked up the 12-gauge and tapped the end of the barrel with his finger.

"They're not mine; I keep them safe for the guys at the hunting club."

"Hunting Club?" Richard posed the question as he had never heard of it before.

"Yes, hunting. It's not really a club, just a weekend get-together when these guys go off and hunt. Usually, around November."

"What do they hunt?"

Peter smiled. "Anything that moves; and sometimes, even themselves, though, that's more accidental than deliberate."

"Explain."

"I don't know if these are facts, or urban legends, or just bullshit made up to frighten the hunters. I may even have read them in the papers, but these are stories that do the rounds most hunting seasons about freak accidents or bad luck. Last year, or maybe the year before, a lad got shot in the back by accident, by his uncle. The uncle had his rifle cocked, ready to shoot, but tripped, the gun went off, and shot the kid. Terrible it was. A real freak accident, one of those Darwin Award stories. I'm not sure what happened to the kid.

"Then there was the one about a guy who was climbing the side of a steep hill and saw a black snake ahead of him. Instead of letting it go or avoiding it, he approached it, and banged the butt of his rifle down on the snake's head. Missed the snake, the butt hit the ground, the force of the blow fired the rifle, and blew his head off. Now that's really freaky. But as I said, it maybe just be an urban myth, or at least worthy of one of those stupid Awards."

"So, you got these guns because they didn't want any accidents?"

"You could say that. Both of them are Cypriots, with families, and they don't want the kids getting their hands on them, or their wives finding out. I think they told them they had BB guns, harmless air rifles. But these 12-gauges can do a lot of damage. You ever use one?"

"No, never a shot-gun, just the standard rifle. Although, I did fire a pistol a couple of times when we were in training. I can't remember the last time I fired a gun."

"It's something you never forget, and when the time comes, you will remember how to do it."

"Where did these guys get the guns from anyway?"

"I think the shot-gun was bought, but the service pistol, he probably kept from his army days. They still have conscription here for the kids coming out of school. Sometimes, it's two years, maybe less. The men who've done their army duty must go back once every six months, sometimes more, for refresher training. Which is a real pain if you are self-employed and lose money for the day. I knew a couple of guys who ran their own business and had to report back, or they could be fined. At times, quite heavily. One of them used to drive a tank, so he was always in demand." Peter watched Richard, as he brandished the shot-gun. "Do you think you will be able to use the guns then?"

Richard raised the 12-Gauge to his shoulder, and took aim.

Peter approved his stance, held up his beer bottle again, and chinked it against Richard's as he lowered the shot-gun. "Cheers."

When Jenny arrived at Larnaca airport, the departure lounge was not too busy, hence why only a couple of aisles were open. She waited for the two or three passengers in front of her to move down the roped-off line towards the desks. Ahead of her she could see a small family group, a young boy, girl, and a Mum and Dad. She thought she recognised them, but wasn't sure.

"Thank you, Mr and Mrs Kelly, have a good flight." The girl at the desk didn't recognise the family either, and perhaps that was just as well.

They collected their boarding passes and made their way to the departure gate.

Jenny checked in.

"I'm going to call Julie. Maybe we can go out later to have something to eat. My treat."

"Fine, but I'm going for a nap first. I suggest you do the same."

"No sleep for me, thanks, I will just call and wait for you to wake up!" Sleep meant dreams and he never knew what his held and was not willing to risk it. He picked up the phone, walked with it into his bedroom, sat on the bed, dialled the number, and waited.

"Hello." Julie's voice was clear, in fact, as if she were standing by the door.

"Hi, Jules." He wanted to say more but waited for her reply.

"Hi, darling. How are you? We had a really busy day yesterday, what with Simon and the kids. Molly and Matthew got on Skype and we spent about an hour talking to them. It was nice. They said they are having a great time, even if their jobs are hard work, but fun. One of the para-sailing guys had an accident and Matthew was asked to take over and drive the boat, he loves it. Molly thinks she might quit her job and look for a receptionist's position in one of the posh hotels. I suspect they'll spend most of the summer there before going on to Australia or New Zealand."

His eyes filled with tears, his throat became dry, and his voice unable to formulate speech. He just listened, to the words of his wife, the words that he so desperately needed to hear. It didn't matter how trivial the conversation was, he needed to hear her, needed to hold her, and above all, he needed to tell her he loved her. But he couldn't do any of those things, all he could do was listen.

"…so, what's happening with you? Are you nearly finished?"

He cleared his throat, trying to make his reply as normal as possible even though he was breaking inside. "We could be finished after tomorrow. They might have a decision by then. Things have been a little difficult."

"I can imagine. I heard about the boat sinking. All those wedding guests, most of them Brits too, all over the papers here." Julie's skill for the pragmatic was well-practiced. "Tomorrow… That's good. So, you could be back by Thursday?" She was looking for confirmation.

"Yes, love, will try for Thursday. Just have a couple more things to do."

"Okay. Talk to you before you leave then. Love you, take care."

He was about to tell her, "Love you" back, but the line cut off, leaving the last words he needed her to know hanging in mid-air. He put the phone down, buried his head in the bed sheet, and let his tears flow freely.

Rycinne had spent the best part of half an hour collating her tapes and at the same time going through some phrase books searching for the word Richard had used, σκότος, one she was unfamiliar with. She went online and typed it in the best way she knew as she was unsure of its spelling in Greek/English, which created a backlash of hugely differing responses.

But she had to know for certain what the word meant, so she called her friend Agostino. He was a college lecturer and well-versed in languages. She wrote the word down the best she could phonetically spell it.

He confirmed, almost instantly, that σκότος (skotos) was ancient Greek, and it meant darkness.

She would call Peter later and tell him what she had found out, but first, she needed to finish her filing. As she continued filing she couldn't quite get out of her head that morning's session. Richard was a great example of a man suffering from PTSD, but there was something else about him, something much darker and mysterious, something she did not yet understand, or could quite put her finger on.

CHAPTER TWENTY-TWO

Last Supper

Paphos, late evening

The guys dressed casually for their last night together. At least, that was Richard's take on things. He wanted to avoid becoming too maudlin when it came to conversation, but it was difficult to dismiss entirely. Phrases like "the condemned man ate a healthy breakfast, or in this case, supper" came to mind. But the meal went some way to easing the atmosphere.

They had chosen a Greek Restaurant called *Stavros* which, according to the billboard outside, "Delights its customers with traditional Cypriot mezes". This particular variety, according, again, to the billboard, had some "twenty-five dishes for 20 Euros" which was exceptionally good value under the present financial climate.

Taking a corner table at the back of the restaurant, they ordered their customary large beers and began to relax. And almost as soon as they settled into their seats with their drinks, the dishes came thick and fast. First course was the Greek salad, followed by Halloumi and Lounza, and Keftedes (vine leaves) wrapped around ground beef and minced vegetables.

As they tucked into the first of the dishes, a couple of young women in their early thirties arrived, sat close to their table, and Peter was quick to notice how they kept glancing at them. He smiled back at the younger-looking of the two, who wore a twin set of white shirt and pants, decorated with some shiny bright orange beads. Her top was open to the second button and her tanned skin glistened under the bright candlelight.

Her friend wore a short red miniskirt, which gave a great view of her well-tanned legs, but unlike her friend, her top was more conservative; more of a blouse, neatly buttoned, with just the top one open. Both were brunettes and already had good tans, so they were either locals, or sun worshippers.

Richard didn't pay much attention to either of them, as he dived back into the Greek salad and pushed his fork into the newly arrived Luganica sausages, delightfully tinged with a hint of red wine. Peter on the other hand, continued to play eye-to-eye games with the girl in white directly across from the table.

Perhaps it was just the distraction Peter needed, but for Richard, it only reminded him how much he missed Julie and how much he wanted to be back with her. To change the subject and to take his mind off the blossoming situation between his friend and his possible companion, Richard decided to tell him about his plan for the following day. Only, he would change one crucial detail. "Pete, it's tomorrow."

"Are you sure? How do you know?"

"Let's call it intuition. I suspect she will be waiting, whatever time I turn up anyway, so tomorrow seems as good a time as any. I will make this decision, not her."

"When tomorrow?" Peter glanced across as the women ordered a good bottle of Claret, and waited for the waiter to pour the taster for the older of the two; the one with the red skirt, the one he had chosen for Richard.

"It will be at midnight, just as it was before. Therefore, I suggest we get some well-deserved sleep during the day and try to rest in preparation."

"Seems like a good idea. But tonight, as it could be our last, why don't we party? These two look like they are in the mood. She just put down that glass of wine in two gulps."

"I think you might have a better chance than me, so if you want to ask them for a drink, why not?" Richard felt he owed Peter something out of the night, having already lied to him.

"Tell you what, let's get through these mezes and then we'll see what the evening holds. Bar Street is a good starter, although, I think some of the clubs there might be a bit on the young side, and we look like a couple of old swingers."

"Swingers?" Richard smiled and chuckled at the idea of the two of them throwing in their car keys for a couple of like-minded strangers.

"Oh, fuck it, Rich, you know what I mean. I thought boring old farts was a bit too near the mark."

"Cheers."

They touched glasses for the second time that night and raised them to the two young women. The response was reciprocated. Maybe, just maybe, they were onto a good thing.

Larnaca

It was quiet at the hospital; the night shift had just clocked on and most of the patients in the wards were already asleep. Elena sat in the hospital café, her paperwork was up to date, and all the autopsies completed. She had worked like a Trojan these past few days and desperately needed to get away for a few days. If only she had her man to go with her. If only.

Paphos, Bar Street

The evening wasn't working out as Peter had envisaged. The two women had agreed to go with them to Bar Street but after a couple of Sex-on-the-Beach Cocktails and a Brandy Sour, Amy, the younger one, found a younger man's company more to her liking, rather than Peter's.

Richard was left to chat with the older woman, Barbara, whom, turned out to be an interesting person. She had worked for the UN in Nicosia but was now a translator running her own business. She had only recently moved to Paphos and lived near Coral Bay. Her friend had an apartment nearby but had just lost her job working for a real estate agent. Barbara seemed settled but Amy was looking at returning to the UK.

It was all good conversation as it took his mind off the day ahead, even if for a short while, but with Peter's nose out of joint, Richard felt he needed to move on and take his brooding friend with him. After their goodbyes, they left the bar, the music totally unintelligible to both, with its blaring, crashing, and banging against their ears.

CHAPTER TWENTY-THREE
Subterfuge and Submission

Paphos, Tuesday

The previous night's supper and impromptu date with the girls had proven just one thing, how ordinary life was. Given that this was the eve of destruction, there were no trumpets or fanfare or exorbitant and elaborate ceremonies. All it took was a good meal, with a good friend, and a bit of flirting. It made Richard feel good inside, but today, it would all change. One way or another, destiny was about to come knocking at his door and he had to let it in.

Peter came out of his room nursing a hangover, which he had nurtured through drinking beer, red wine, vodka, and several assorted cocktails and the obligatory Zivania. The one sensible thing he did was to leave the car at the restaurant and the walk back to the house helped him with his tipsy demeanour. However, the aftereffects were not leaving soon enough and he searched the cupboard and kitchen drawers for a packet of aspirin; the best cure he knew for self-inflicted damage.

Whilst Peter plodded about the villa, Richard sat quietly on the patio. He had made a fresh pot of coffee and was savouring it slowly, while his phone was switched on, so he could keep checking for messages every few minutes. He also kept looking at his watch, noticing how the hands did not move as fast as he would like. There was no rush to die, or whatever fate awaited him, but he had to be sure Peter was out-of-the-way before he made his move. The car, having been left at the restaurant, presented him with the perfect opportunity to put his plan into action.

Peter joined him on the patio. The day was bright and the sunshine hot as they drank their coffee together. He picked up one of the Scylla's pictures, pushed a pen through the image, and grinned. "We are coming to get you, bitch."

Richard smiled back and thought, *'if only it were that easy'*. "Sure you're feeling okay? Are you ready and fit? You know we can't afford any mistakes, especially as we don't know what we're up against. So far, it has all been supposition, but today we learn the truth of what we are facing. I need to know you are ready."

"I have never been more ready in my life. I'm as good as I was twenty years ago, when we were first on that copter."

"And today, we are going back to that very place. We meet the goddess where it all began, and hopefully, where it will all end, so I suggest..." Richard paused. "What's the time?"

Both men looked at their watches simultaneously.

"In true army fashion, synchronise watches. 3.2.1. Mark... 13:36."

"Christ, is it that late?" Peter looked again at his watch.

"Yes, it is, I suggest we get some brunch or lunch and go back to bed for a few hours."

"Nice idea but you can bloody well forget a fry up, matey. I'm sticking with black coffee, you have whatever you want."

"Tea and toast is fine for me. Oh, where are the car keys, I can go pick it up, as I need to get some fresh air. And for your peace of mind, I am insured to drive anywhere in the world, took out a policy last year."

"Fine, the keys are in the pot there. But be careful, these Cypriots drive like... you don't need me to tell you. Just be careful and watch out for the cops, who hide in bus stops. Do you know how to find Stavros Restaurant? We parked just along from there. A reminder, I activated the alarm so turn it off before alerting the entire island. Right, that's me finished, and as you say, off to bed. I feel another one of my headaches coming on."

"Leave it to me, I'll get the car and then join you, though, not in the biblical sense."

"I should bloody well hope not." Peter grinned and laughed loudly as he returned to his bedroom.

Part one of Richard's plan was in place, part two was just beginning. He waited for Peter's door to close, then opened the sports bag where the guns were stowed in. He took out the service pistol, checked it then placed it back in the bag, making sure the safety was on. Then he took out a clip, which he also checked, before sliding the bag back under the chair.

As he moved quietly past Peter's door, he could hear him snoring loudly. Richard opened his own bedroom door and went to his wardrobe, took out a plain short-sleeved white shirt, removed his somewhat faded "Cyprus Rocks" T-shirt, and replaced it with the short-sleeved one before walking back into the lounge.

The clock on the wall said 2:30pm, he had just under four hours to get everything in place. But right this moment he would just shut his eyes and try to get forty winks. Before dozing off, he set his alarm for 4:30pm. It would be enough time for him to pick up the car and drive to Petra Tou Romiou.

Nicosia

Two more committee meetings and a lunch saw Panayotis back in his office, pondering on what his next move should be. The British Embassy and The Cypriot Government had agreed to a deal with a commercial airliner, so the bodies would be repatriated by the end of the week.

The rest of the walking wounded and those with minor injuries were due to return on the same flight on Friday, which gave Panayotis three days to assemble all the necessary protocols needed and offer some sort of explanation for the tragedy, despite the glaring fact that he still had no idea what had caused it.

He was however, steering himself increasingly towards mechanical engine failure, which could support some of the reasons behind the disaster, but certainly not all. The extensive injuries and wounds suffered by some of the passengers could not be explained away by the boat coming apart, yet there was no other logical explanation. Anything else was stepping over the boundaries of reality and into fantasy, and that was something Panayotis, or the island, could not afford to do.

Already, investors were starting to raise concerns. If the bail-out and repercussions of that decision were not bad enough, these events were weighing heavy on the consciences and bank balances of those who still had a vested interest in promoting the island and its attractions. Anything untoward or inexplicable could further jeopardise any chance of recovery, or be seen as the final straw, and the beginning of financial genocide. Whatever happened from now on, Panayotis and his colleagues had to get it right, for all their sakes.

Richard woke before the alarm went off. He got up quickly, his new white shirt slightly creased from the sleeping position, and removed his shoes so as not to make a noise as he tiptoed past Peter's door. Peter still snored loudly, blowing out of his mouth and nose in a sort of chorus; a peculiar sound, for as one snore finished it led straight into another as if being joined in a harmony of snorts.

He peeped inside, reached behind the door, and grappled for the key, which was in the keyhole. He gingerly pulled it out, careful not to disturb the sleeping beauty. Gently, he inserted the key on the outside and turned it, locking the door again. Then for good measure, he took a chair from the kitchen and prised it under the handle. "That should work." He whispered to himself, confident that his mate was safely locked away. As he left Peter's room, he would swear that his snoring was getting louder.

Stepping back into the lounge, he pulled the bag from under the chair, and picked out the pistol and clip; he zipped the bag closed again and pushed it back under the chair. He found the small pot where the car keys were and put them in his pocket, then grabbed a small white plastic bag, and placed the weapon inside. He looked around the room one last time, before opening the front door, and closing it quietly behind him.

The car was about a ten-minute walk away, so he moved swiftly down the street, crossing out from the cul-de-sac to the beach road. He checked his watch again; it read ten to five. He needed to quicken the pace, as it would probably take him just under an hour to get where he needed to be. He thought about calling Julie, but resisted the impulse, and kept walking.

Within a few more minutes, he spotted the car, which was still safe and secure. Getting closer, he pressed the alarm button and the lights flashed intermittently on the front and back as he opened the door. He climbed inside, put on his seatbelt, adjusted the mirror, and started it. The engine purred as he revved slowly, not to draw attention to himself, then indicated, and eased into the road. There was no one about so he spun the wheels into a U-turn, and placed his foot down on the accelerator. The clock on the dashboard read 5:25. His watch was slow.

He took the road down towards the main roundabout at Kato Pafos, before turning left, and followed the sign to Limassol and Nicosia. He eased his way through the automatic gearbox and drove at a steady fifty, careful to avoid any possible police action. He crossed over two roundabouts before hitting the highway, a road he knew very well, and accelerated.

Rycinne had been busy with three clients and had not yet had time to call Peter. Then as she sat in her apartment drinking a tall glass of lemon tea, she decided now was the time to do so. Peter's number was on speed dial, so she waited for him to reply.

Peter woke suddenly from his slumber, a tinge of hangover still forming most of the reason his head felt woozy and light-headed. He picked up his phone and noticed who it was. "Hi, Rycinne. Sorry to keep you, late night."

"Late afternoon by the sound of it. Are you okay?"

"Yes, yes, fine. What can I do for you?"

"Remember I said I would find out about that word Richard used? It turns out it's ancient Greek, and means darkness. I don't know if that makes any sense to you, or him. How is he by the way?"

"He's fine, better than me, didn't drink as much as I did. Darkness you say, and it's ancient Greek? Thanks for the information, I'll tell him. So, coffee next week?"

"Looking forward to it. You know, if I didn't know better I would say Richard has some Greek blood in him somewhere. Anyway, take it easy and don't forget to tell him, darkness. Bye, Peter."

"Bye, Rycinne, take care." Peter placed his phone on the bed, rubbed his eyes and hair as if trying to wake himself, then stood up, with traces of a muffled drum banging in his temple.

He walked over to the door and turned the handle, it was locked. He looked at his watch, 5:20. He tried the handle again but the door refused to move. At once he realised what was happening. Richard had locked him in and it was clear that whatever he was going to do, he planned on doing alone. "Oh no, matey, that's what you think."

Peter took three paces back and shoved hard against the door, it wouldn't budge. He stepped back again and pressed harder with his shoulder then slammed it into the wood. "Fuck you, Richard."

He went into his wardrobe and pulled out a heavy pair of boots. Slipping on a pair of socks and the boots, he stepped back again, raised one leg, and launched a ferocious kick against the door handle, which buckled and split the wood around it. He slammed his foot hard against the handle a second time and the door cracked open. Wood splinters and a scattered shattered door handle littered the floor as the kitchen chair spilled across the passageway.

Peter ran into the lounge, grabbed the bag with the shotgun, and slung it over his shoulder. Forgetting about the discussion about the car keys, he scrounged around for a minute. When it dawned on him that Richard had them, he opened a couple of sideboard drawers and pulled out a small tin box; on the front were two letters etched in the metal, HD. He opened it, almost reverently, and took out another set of keys. He threw them into his shorts' pocket, put his denim bomber-jacket on, and hurried towards the back door, slamming it behind him.

Going to the side of the villa, he opened the garage door, and saw the clean black tarpaulin that covered what he was looking for. He pulled the material away and gleaming underneath was the most beautiful Harley-Davidson customised creation he had ever seen, complete with hog handlebars, shimmering chrome, and silver bodywork. This 'Chopper' was not just an executive toy, it was the culmination of a dream, one that he was about to ride.

"God bless you, Tony K." He mumbled to himself as he kissed the top of the fuel tank and leaned down to the ignition. If Richard was meeting his goddess today, he was making sure there was an angel going there with him, albeit a somewhat middle-aged and slightly overweight one.

He started the 'Chopper', placed the helmet, styled like an SS Stormtrooper's, on his head, and listened as the engine breathed in. As he pulled the throttle, she exhaled, and a puff of white smoke followed his trail as he exited the garage.

Richard slowed down and pulled into the car park at Petra Tou Romiou. Costas' restaurant and coffee bar had been his local haunt when he was at the rocks before, and from appearances, it still kept the crowds fed and watered, despite the famous rocks not being there anymore as picture subjects.

He looked around and noticed the parking lot was not too busy; some of the people were returning from the beach and putting their towels, bags, and other paraphernalia into the boots of their cars.

He opened the plastic bag in which he kept the pistol and clip and took a peek inside. Carefully, he transferred the clip into the pistol and waited for the click. With the clip installed safely, he drew the gun out of the bag, checking that no one was about as he tucked it into the back of his jeans, then made sure the tail of his white short-sleeved shirt covered the shape.

Climbing out of the car, he began a slow walk towards the beach; the sun was low in the sky and beginning its last-minute preparations for setting. Richard avoided eye contact with the last few stragglers coming up the path, as the sun seemed to suddenly drop quickly, almost out of synch with nature.

His footsteps moved him closer to the roadside and he crossed the asphalt, taking a small step over the crash-barrier and down the cliff-side that led to the beach. Reaching the base of the cliff, he felt a shudder, just as if he had been pushed, the surrealism of his fate unfolding before him.

"So, Mr Cole, you have decided to join me." The goddess spoke from the shore's edge. "You will come to me with not a trapping from the life you have led. Anything that you wear must be discarded before you reach this hallowed spot where I stand. Do you understand? And when you reach me, you will go on your knees and beg me to take you as my slave, is that understood? Poor Richard, if you had made the right choice, this would not have been necessary."

Richard bowed his head and reached his hand behind his back, to check the pistol was still there. He needed to get closer to get a better shot.

"The sun is setting now. Once he does, you will come to me."

He stood listening to her words for a moment and nodded agreement then nearing the top of the beach, he looked behind him and noticed a cloud of purple smoke descending from the hills and waft down to act like a curtain to block all views from the road.

Moving closer, a pair of Doric columns appeared before him and on either side of these, small bushes of Myrtle blossomed and shed their petals on the ground. As he stepped slowly forward, he looked down to see the space between the columns covered with a carpet of leaves. The aroma from the Myrtle bushes hung heavily in the air and as he knelt between the two columns, he picked one of the leaves that lay strewn everywhere.

These were laurel, and as he turned to look behind him, the misty veil had nestled over the cliff side's shoulders. Emerging from the haze were two smartly dressed figures; the first, he recognised as Christoulides, and the second also looked familiar. As they continued walking towards him, Richard realised it was Mr Lakis from the airport.

"Before you take another step, I need to speak with you." Lukas, aka Zeus, stopped just a few feet away.

His companion, stood beside him, holding a slim black attaché case in his hand.

Richard turned to face them, keeping his gun well hidden.

"You know Mr. Lakis, he works for me. And let's give him his real name. Aeolus, Keeper of the Winds."

Richard smiled. "I suppose you know many others who are not who they say they are. But now is not the time to discuss this. As you can see, I am about to meet your daughter."

Zeus stepped forward, ignoring the comment, then took another five paces and stood at the base of one of the columns.

"You have come to see the show, Father?" Aphrodite smiled at Zeus.

"No, daughter, I have come to plead for this mortal's life and soul. He is not what you want, merely a substitute for your own true love. The one you really want, you can't have, because he is gone! Can you not see that? Can you not see that all you have done has been worthless? He is not the one and he will not come to you willingly, he will only do so because you threaten his family, and he is prepared to sacrifice himself for them. The mayhem you have caused is evil and comes from a woman who is bitter and hurt, not the Daughter I love and honour. We have all lost loved ones, I know this pain, but this, is not right. You must let him go back to the life that is his, not the life you demand of him."

"Have you finished, Father? Your words, like you, no longer possess any conviction or authority. But my word is power and I will show you." Aphrodite turned towards the water and the waves began to thrash and crash on the shore, sending turrets of white horses high into the sky as the Scylla emerged from the surf.

The creature stood ten to twelve-feet above the waves, its arms, legs, and tentacles all moving together as if swaying to a silent rhythm. The cries from the canines buried in her abdomen rang out across the beach, the face of the creature serene and beautiful, her image personified in a complete 'yin and yang' of the monster.

Richard stumbled back, the pictures, the images; none of them did this thing justice.

"This is my power, Father. With my sister here, I can do as I wish. No man or god can stop me and you know it. So, enough with this petty begging. Cole is mine, and I will have him."

Richard stepped forward, his fate sealed, as Zeus stepped away. He nodded his thanks to the old man, removed his shoes and socks, and took his first tentative steps down the green carpet to his destiny.

CHAPTER TWENTY-FOUR

Redemption and Resurrection

His bare feet trod gingerly upon the laurel leaves underfoot, and he felt them crackle softly between his toes. As he passed the first set of columns, another pair appeared, flanked again by Myrtle bushes. He moved slowly another two paces and more columns appeared. As he drew closer to the shore, he reached up to his shirt buttons and began to undo them slowly.

The goddess moved two steps forward, trying to get a better look at the man as he approached.

Christoulides and Lakis could only watch helplessly as Richard progressed down the carpet.

Passing another set of columns with his shirt fully open, he peeled it off and saw Aphrodite's eyes as she scrutinised his every movement.

The Scylla slithered closer to the shoreline.

Peter edged the motorcycle into the side of the café, jumped off, and took the shot-gun from the bag. He glanced around, good, no one was about, and ran across the road. He peered down to the beach and saw Richard walking slowly towards the water.

As if by design, the mist enveloping the roadside began descending rapidly in front of Peter, and to escape the approaching obstruction, he leapt over the barrier, through the cloud, and into another, and different world.

All Peter knew, rationalised, doubted or believed in, was captured in that instant as he saw Richard's fantasies come alive. As he skirted down the cliff, he too saw the Doric columns, the carpet of leaves, the two smartly dressed men standing as witnesses, the goddess at the edge of the shoreline, and the Scylla, as vile and repugnant as he could ever have imagined.

Richard, bare-chested and bare-footed, moved unhurriedly down the verdant carpet towards the goddess, and estimated he was about twenty-five-feet before he would reach her. There was also just one more piece of clothing to remove. Edging closer, he started to pull open the top button on his jeans.

She too drew closer; he was teasing her as she watched him strip.

Peter ran down the slope, shouting, and yelling for all he was worth.

The unexpected distraction created surprise and slight panic on those who heard his banshee-cry as he screeched wildly at the Scylla. "You mother…"

He fired a shot directly into the centre of the creature, the blast creating a gaping hole in one of the canine's heads as the full impact exploded into her gut. Crimson splashes and sinew spurted and spewed from the stomach.

Reaching into the back of his pants, Richard took the pistol out, and unloaded five shots into the torso, neck, and shoulders of the Scylla.

Aphrodite screamed, as her pet of death writhed in agony, and felt her own power diminish with each slowing heartbeat of the creature.

The Scylla whipped, lashed, smashed, and slashed its tentacles towards Peter as he sent another volley into her body.

Richard had one shot left and he was going to make it count. But as he aimed, the creature's whip tentacle caught him on the leg. His flesh opened and he fell back. Lying on the ground, he pointed the gun at Aphrodite.

She saw his movement and stood still.

He raised the pistol to aim at her… his hand started shaking, as if someone had grabbed the gun and was holding it down. He fired at the ground in front of her, the bullet embedding itself in the sand. He slumped back.

With the Scylla reeling, Peter loaded again, and fired twice.

The shells burst into her skin, tearing her flesh open, and ripping her insides apart. She slipped into the water, nursing her wounds.

Aphrodite began to weep and whimper, sensing her power diminishing.

Zeus stepped forward, motioned to Aeolus, and commanded. "Send that creature to where it belongs."

Aeolus opened his attaché case, took out a canvas bag, and from it, all the power of the winds. Cradling them gently in his palms, he then unleashed a vortex towards the Scylla that sucked her in, and cast her to the four winds.

Peter had also suffered a hit and was bleeding, but not as much as his friend, who lay still on the ground at the base of the last column.

Zeus, Aeolus, and Peter gathered close to Richard. His wound was deep and blood gushed out. They had to stop the bleeding before he lost too much.

Richard opened his eyes weakly. His focus on Peter, he nodded his thanks, and whispered. "You did it, pal, you did it." His eyes closed.

Peter grabbed hold of him, cradling him in his arms, and using the discarded shirt, tried to stem the bleeding.

Zeus and Aeolus looked on helplessly while Aphrodite knelt by the water's edge distraught, tears of self-pity streaming down her face.

Blood flowed continuously from Richard, who was losing consciousness fast, even as Peter held onto him. The blood oozed from the deep wound, running freely, and his tanned red face began to lose its colour as he opened his eyes again.

Peter looked to the heavens. "Somebody do something." Tears welled in his eyes as he watched his friend slip slowly away.

As his breathing became slow and laboured, Richard began to shiver. A small dribble of dark blood, almost indigo in colour, slipped from his lips. "She is waiting for me… I can see her, she is calling me."

"Who is?"

"She says her name is Fate, and is dressed all in black. Says she has been waiting for me for a long time."

"Stay with me, Richard. We'll get you out of here, and all fixed up." Peter drew him closer, his entire body covered in Richard's blood. He looked up at the two men who could offer no consolation. "Can't you do something?" He pleaded, but got no help.

Aphrodite, still a small distance away, stood staring at the man whom she had coveted, her expression almost nonchalant as she watched him slip from life.

"Σκότος…" Richard's last word verified his passing.

Aphrodite turned, and raced towards Richard. "What did he say?"

Her Father spoke, "σκότος."

Her scream and tears echoed around the columns and rocks as she fell to the ground, clutching at Richard's body "No, No, NOOO…"

Her words only added confusion to the scene unfolding, because as Richard's blood streamed from his body, the liquid became solid, forming small white petals of anemone flowers, which turned blood-red and spread like a carpet across the shore and beach.

Aphrodite fell beside the body of her lover and spoke in whispers in ancient Greek. "Αυτό δεν έπρεπε να συμβεί, Θεέ μου, ο Άδωνις μου, επιστρέψτε σε μένα να επιστρέψω."

The bewilderment and astonished look on the faces of those on the beach, ratified what was happening. Richard had died, shedding his mortal skin, to become the person he had always been, the god Adonis, Aphrodite's lover in another time.

She held Adonis' limp body, cradling him against her, holding and embracing him as her one true love, the one she knew all along was hers.

Peter looked to Zeus for an explanation, not knowing who he was. "How is this possible? What just happened? Somebody tell me what is going on." He looked to Lukas again beseechingly.

"You want answers, I can only tell you what I know and it will be hard enough for you to believe. Your friend is not whom you think he is. In his human form, he is Richard Cole, but as Aphrodite's lover he is the god Adonis. She knew that from the moment he was sent to war and asked for her to *"bring him back safe"* That was the trigger, the signal.

"She knew then who he really was, when he asked her to bring him back safely, and the reason was, Adonis did this every time he went into battle or hunting. The one time he didn't ask her, was the day he died. She never forgave herself for that, for not bestowing her blessing on him.

"Adonis is the one god who has the power of resurrection so it was just a matter of time, she thought, when he would be hers again. But she was wrong, for when the choice to live as god or mortal came, he chose the mortal life and elected to live as Richard Cole. His humanity outweighed his divinity, and it was for him better to live as a man than a god. His love for his wife and family was just too strong. I know it's difficult to grasp, because even I don't fully understand it.

"She did all she could to make him love her again and choose her. She penetrated his dreams, offering sanctuary to his nightmares, she pursued him like a possessed lover until Cole was finally forced to make his choice. His one true love, the woman in his dreams, or his wife. He chose his wife. That was the bitterest of all rejections for her.

"Cole never knew until now about his other self, as there were never any clues to his identity. He chose to live in the mortal world, growing up as a mortal. It was Richard who found her, remember? He found her image in the sea. When he did that, it was for her just a matter of time before he realised who he really was. But that never happened, his deity remained a secret until today, and now in his death, his true self is revealed. That is why she is calling to the spirit world to bring him back safe to her, as he always asked of her."

"Can't you do anything?" Peter begged, tears in his eyes. Then he sat on the sand, with the gods of mythology around him, and the lifeless body of his dear friend in his arms. He had no more words.

"Yes, I can. It is time for me to put things back as they were, Mr Shaw."

"You said he was the god of resurrection, will he come back?"

"That, I do not know, it is for the Fates to decide. But you go now, and do not look back or open your eyes." Zeus moved closer to the water, past the grieving Aphrodite, and stood with Aeolus.

Peter hurried to the top of the slope, took one last look back, and saw the two figures at the shore, now joined by a third one. He wasn't altogether sure, but it looked like the old man from the bookshop. He passed through the mist curtain.

Zeus reached into his pocket, took out a small silver pen, pulled the top off, and stretched it out until it was about a foot long. The light from the piece dazzled and lit the entire setting in a brilliant whiteness that hurt the eyes.

He turned to his two companions. "When I give the word, I want you, Aeolus, and you, Poseidon, to use your powers to control the elements." He stood with his arms outstretched and with the silver bolt in his hand, slammed it down into the sand. "NOW."

The rumble and trembling was felt underfoot as the sea began to expand and the wind howled and ravaged the heavens. The noise grew louder and louder with every thunderclap and flash of lightning as the forces of nature fought for supremacy with the gods of old. The waves wrestled with the winds and joined together to lash against the shore.

Zeus held his ground, even as Aeolus pulled out his bag and began to battle the tempest. The force of the storm was so violent that the earth shook and fissures appeared along the shoreline.

The cage that housed the image of the goddess shattered and scattered as Poseidon moved into the water, bent down, and took from the seabed his trident, which he held in his right hand and extended across the briny surface. With his arms outstretched, he controlled the waves.

As the sea subsided and with it, the winds calmed, the rumble from below ground signalled the rising of Aphrodite's Rocks from the depths. First, the small one, then the second, and finally the largest and most majestic of them.

Zeus had come through, The Rocks of Aphrodite were restored, and the questions would soon begin as to how it was possible.

"It is done. Thank you, my brothers, it's time we left this place. There will be much talk about what has occurred and we should not be seen here. But before we go, I have one request. Poseidon, will you take care of my daughter? She needs your love now. Once, you swore to me that you would protect her always, so today, I ask that of you."

Poseidon moved forward and without saying a word, took Aphrodite by the hand and together they walked into the ocean.

Zeus turned towards the body lying on the sand. Its transformation was complete. Adonis was gone and the lifeless body of Richard Cole lay there.

"As for you, Mr Cole, I will see that you are honoured and respected in the way you deserve. Man, or god, you are one of the bravest and most courageous I have ever known."

Peter never saw what happened below or heard those words, the people on the shore had vanished. The mist cleared and looking back across the beach, he saw the place as it had always been, with Aphrodite's Rock restored to the island.

The sound of sirens and police cars interrupted his solemn contemplation as the first of many hundreds of people began running towards the new phenomenon. He climbed back onto the motorcycle and rode off; not into the sunset, but into a new and unknown dawn.

CHAPTER TWENTY-FIVE

Requiem for a Hero

Three months passed since Richard died. Peter's call to Julie was the most harrowing and difficult thing he ever had to do.

The premise of Richard's death was that he was killed by a hit and run driver in Paphos. There were no witnesses, and the police had found no evidence of the perpetrator.

The autopsy was quick and his body was sent to Larnaca. Elena Petrakis performed the ceremony and it was agreed that he would be repatriated at the same time as the others. Instead of ten coffins returning to the UK, there were eleven.

Richard's death may have had more significance if it had not been for the re-emergence of the rocks at Petra Tou Romiou. The chaos the tremors caused, and the subsequent appearance of the rocks generated a surge of activity from every corner of the globe. Geologists, seismologists, volcanologists… there seemed to be a scientist for every 'ology' or discipline known to creation, and with every scientist, there were at least three media or journalists following the story as it unfolded day by day.

One theory was that the rocks were like a new island being formed, that the earthquake that accompanied the storm had in some way shifted the rocks from the ocean and forced them to rise again. It was pure conjecture but for many, it seemed to suffice.

The site was closed off, as the engineers and scientists went about their job. But the publicity it had created meant that the island was now crammed with visitors of every nation, and who wanted to see this new wonder of the ancient world as soon as possible.

Peter flew back with Richard's body. Julie called the children and they returned to the UK.

The English press gave him more coverage than the Cypriots had. In fact, the day the rocks appeared, Richard's death produced only one small column in the paper. Whether the Cypriots wanted to keep his visit quiet was anyone's guess, but Peter suspected that Mr Christoulides might have had a hand in the matter.

Richard Cole was buried in a cemetery just outside of Aldershot. A few of his old army pals also turned up, and as a last gesture, one brought a recording of the last post, which they played across his coffin. Peter tried to give the Eulogy but was so distressed that Richard's brother Simon stepped in to support him.

Julie was one of the last to leave the graveside, scattering white rose petals over his final resting place as silent tears rolled down her face. As she stood by the grave, Peter stood next to her, placed his arm around her shoulders, and saluted his best friend.

Matthew and Molly joined them, and held their Mother in their arms. Then gently, together with Peter, all three steered her back to the car. Peter spoke briefly to Matthew before he left them. Then, the funeral car started and Julie and her children got into the back seat; together they set about building a new life for the Cole family.

Panayotis had a new challenge. The rocks would provide every possibility of prosperity and bring about a complete renaissance for the island. It was another string added to his already expanding bow, and with more developments in oil and gas taking place every day, the island's prospects were bright, and the tragic events of recent months, quickly pushed aside. True, there were still ongoing inquiries, but no longer with as much verve as before. Other events had overtaken them, which is always the way in politics.

Peter tried to settle back in Cyprus but found it difficult. Besides, Tony K was planning to return within the next couple of weeks and although he asked him to stay, Peter declined. He needed something else in his life, not just memories. Sheila had an offer for the house and accepted it, so he might get something from the sale, if she felt generous.

As Peter sat drinking his chilled Keo, he tried to put into perspective all that had happened, trying to make sense of it. How he had become involved from the beginning, with the trip on the helicopter out to the Gulf, then the reunion and the rocks' discovery, and now the revelation that his best friend wasn't whom he thought he was. The irony was that Richard Cole had never wanted to be a hero. But apparently, even he couldn't stop it from happening.

The phone on the table rang once. Peter didn't recognise the number but opened the message anyway. It read,

"Mr Shaw, I am sorry we never really introduced ourselves, but the day was a little difficult. I wanted to tell you that my daughter has returned to where she should be, and that a good friend of ours is looking after her. Yasso, Mr Shaw. Z"

Peter read the text again, "My Daughter has returned to where she should be… Daughter?" His mind whirled for a couple more seconds, before he clicked the image that had also been sent.

It showed the rock of Aphrodite, the one Richard had first seen with her image. Next to it was a figure; the head and shoulders of a man, on his head, something that resembled a crown, and in his hand, a trident.

Mr Christoulides, whom he now knew to be Zeus, was true to his word. Poseidon would now guard The Mistress of the Rock.

Like Peter, you can see for yourself. If you believe.

THE END

Many of you will think that Richard Cole's story and his amazing discovery is at an end. You would be wrong!

His tale may be told for now, but his wife Julie's… Well, that is another matter.

In the third part, to discover the truth, she must go right back to the beginning, where it all began, in THE RETURN: Julie's Odyssey.

About the Author

Born in 1952 in Orsett, Essex in England, the youngest son to Welsh parents Iris and Bill Edwards. Upon leaving school, he went into the travel industry, where he travelled the world, working in travel agencies, tour operators and airlines for some 30 years. In 1976 Myron began freelance writing for BBC, radio and television, his credits include The Two Ronnies, Week Ending, and The News Huddlines. In 1980, he joined JWT advertising, as a copywriter writing his first TV commercial for dog food inside 10 days. His love for the creative never left him and in 1987 he created Tubewalking, a new map concept, to help people get around London easier on foot, which still operates today. In 1990 he married Niki, whose family background is Greek Cypriot. On a family trip to Cyprus, visiting Aphrodite's Rock for the first time, the beginnings of his passion to write the story of Mistress of the Rock came into fruition. Moving his family in 2005 to Cyprus to live, gave him the opportunity to write, as during this time he worked on campaigns for TV and Radio in an advertising agency in Limassol. The first manuscript of the book was completed in 2007, released by a local publisher it had a limited audience, but was well received by those who had read it. He has now completed the sequel and is working on the third part of this story. Myron has three children, two sons and one daughter all grown up.

The second book in the trilogy is Scylla: The Revenge

And coming in 2020, Odyssey: Julie's Odyssey

Julie's Odyssey

CHAPTER ONE

Death and clocks

Julie Cole sat alone at the kitchen table sipping her black coffee; she took it extra strong these days. Richard, her husband, was dead; killed during a hit-and-run collision in Cyprus whilst helping his friend Peter. It happened in Paphos, close to Peter's home, and yet, no responsible party had been found. A year might have passed but coming to terms with grief was something she could not do.

Yes, she had her kids and both Matthew and Molly were like emotional bricks, offering vital foundations for her mourning, both strong, sturdy, and resilient, but they too, grieved for their Father, while trying to keep their tears tightly under control, so as not to start their Mother's. But inevitably, tears flowed, triggered by the smallest incidents. A word, a comment, even a look stirred them, as the memories kicked in. She glanced at the hot swirls rising from the cup, just another support she leaned on since Richard's demise.

Peter's phone call about the events was the beginning of a surreal week, as with the passing of days came the slow realisation that Richard was not coming back. Sadly, for all of them, this gradually sunk in.

Since that first day, Julie took to staring at the clock, something she never did before, never paying much attention to the object that had always been there. It had a large wooden case, with distinctive brass hands, and large Roman numerals. It was there, on the mantelpiece, in the living room. Just a simple item that somehow became significant, as it turned into part of her daily routine and gave her something to occupy her thoughts.

She sat watching the hands move on the face; each simulating her present life. The minute hand moved slowly, the hour hand, even slower, at a crawl until needed, and finally, the second hand rushed through its perpetual circle as it delivered life movements, each depicted in the most simplistic form, tick, tick, tick, its constant rhythm. After all, for Julie, time was all she had left.

Under this canopy of an uncertain future, the Coles began to live again.

Sometimes, when no one was around, she slinked away to her bedroom, opened the wardrobe door, and search out Richard's chunkiest jumper. She grabbed it and pushed her face into the soft fabric, letting her nose catch a breath of his smell. Even now, there was still a remnant that was exclusively him. She would breathe it in deep, like a junky on crack, anxious to drag every last sample in; after which she collapsed upon the bed, hugging the jumper to her body and held it tight, wrapping it around her as if he were still inside that precious piece of clothing.

In this position, she fell asleep, just as her tears filled her eyes and dried against her pillow. Other times, she talked to herself, as if she were speaking to Richard.

'I ironed your shirts today. Mat has taken to wearing them since you are not here, and says he likes the feel of them, that they bring you closer to him. I don't know if that is true but he seems to find it a comfort. I am worried about Molly though, she has lost a lot of her sparkle; she was so bright and bubbly when she was away on her gap year, now, she just looks sad. Richard, I hate you for dying and leaving us like this. Then I stop myself from hating you and start to hate myself for letting you go and for talking me into another one of your crazy ideas, knowing I could never stop you even if I wanted to. That is the hardest part, not having any control over your fate and not being there for you.'

In these phantom-filled tantrums, she drifted towards sleep, where her dreams were always mixed, the pictures and memories always vivid, but when she awoke, she could barely remember them, all mere shadows in her sleep. But one she remembered clearly was the dream she had had since she was a child. It was the nightmare that haunted her continuously.

She always tried to dream through it, but somehow it latched onto her. It began with a noise, a scratching sound that raked across her head, then came a large ball, it was almost translucent and carried within it the sound of voices repeating over and over the words 'of course, of course'. As the ball grew bigger and bigger the words became louder, and from nowhere a pin appeared and moved slowly to burst the billowing ball. It grew closer and the words became louder in her head, 'of course of course' and the pin entered the ball and she expected the ball to burst, but it never did. The pin just kept travelling through and she woke up. She never understood the meaning of the nightmare, or what she should do about it. It had followed her through childhood and now as a woman and mother, it still plagued her.

Most of her dreams included Richard, but recently they had become tinged with other places and faces, some she recognized, some she didn't. The haunting image of Petra Tou Romiou played a backdrop to the scenes unfolding in her subconscious; she saw Peter and Richard, both standing on the shore looking out to sea, as she pushed herself further into the scene she could almost reach out and touch Richard.

She stretched her hand out, calling to him, saw him turn and look towards her then turn back, as the echo of her voice died in the wind only to be replaced by another voice, one she knew well and hoped she would never hear again. Only this time, the voice was calling to her.

'JULIE, JULIE, you must come, you must come. To know the truth, you must come.'